Until We Touch the Stars

For Arcadius 1 - A Tale from the Splintering Empire

LS Derrin

Copyright © 2024 by LS Derrin

All rights reserved.

No portion of this book may be reproduced in any form without written permission from the publisher or author, except as permitted by U.S. copyright law.

Contents

1. Impact — 1
2. Day 0 — 8
3. Day 1 — 15
4. Day 2 — 20
5. Day 3 — 27
6. Day 6 — 37
7. Day 8 — 42
8. Day 11 — 49
9. Day 15 — 55
10. Day 16 — 59
11. Day 18 — 67
12. Day 19 — 74
13. Day 22 — 79
14. Day 25 — 84
15. Day 26 — 92
16. Day 27 — 98
17. Day 28 — 100

18.	Day 29	103
19.	Day 30	104
20.	Day 31	108
21.	Day 34	113
22.	Day 35	118
23.	Day 36	122
24.	Day 37	128
25.	Day 38	132
26.	Day 40	135
27.	Day 45	143
About the author		145

Impact

Greetings to all acting captains! This is a message from the head of the Arcadius Fleet. It is 0500 standard time. Please send in a completed update of your crew evaluation, supply evaluation, and ship evaluation to your wing commander. The Fleet is still on course and on schedule. If you run into any problems, please alert your wing commander at once. We will be reaching Canis Orion within a standard week.

Lieutenant Grace Dillard groaned as the overly chipper Fleet AI, KIR, woke her from a much-needed nap. She sat up in her captain's chair, checking the Prism's position within the Fleet. It was exactly where it had been the entire journey and everything was exactly as expected, as it had been the past several weeks when KIR demanded an update. She did a quick double-check just to be sure before sending in the report to her wing commander.

Then she stretched, debating if it was worth returning to her nap. When she had volunteered to captain the survey shuttle solo, she hadn't realized just how boring it would be. But after spending months in much more crowded quarters with next to no privacy, she decided to make the most of it. She kept the ship neat and tidy, respecting it as if it were her own, even though it wasn't. All lights and sounds were kept within regulation levels, even though most of those rules were put in place out of respect for the rest of the crew. And she kept to all of the expected routines, even though there was no one there to keep her to it.

She ran through all her necessary checks one more time, then switched over to another seat and pulled a book out of the console. Quiet routine had become her friend, and with its help, she was beginning to put a sizable dent in her to-read list as well as finish some classes she had been wanting to take to advance her career whenever they returned home to Arcadius.

Once she settled on her reading for the day and confirmed that her report had gone through, she pulled up one of the many videos her mom had sent her before the Fleet left. Communications had been limited since the Fleet left to deal with the incursion of the Imperials, but her mother had sent her a month's worth of messages to watch whenever she needed something to help stave off the homesickness.

This one was her favorite.

"Honey, you have worked so hard and sacrificed so much to get where you are, and while I am going to miss you, I couldn't possibly be more proud of you. No matter what obstacles life has thrown your way, you never stopped chasing your dreams. There is no doubt in my mind that you are going to continue doing amazing things. I cannot wait to hear about all of your adventures when the Fleet returns. Just remember that no matter what happens, you are the one who makes your future, you are the one who decides who you are. Shoot for the moon and never stop climbing until you touch the stars."

Grace closed her eyes as her mother's words washed over her, soaking them in before she officially started her day.

That's why she never saw it coming.

Lieutenant Dean Lindsay didn't like the quiet much, but being the only person on his small medical skipper meant he could solve that problem however he wished. His solutions tended to involve blasting music typically frowned upon by higher-ups in the Arcadius Fleet, spending hours working through his vast collection of video games and watching movies. On this particular morning as the announcement went out, he was having a little early morning dance party with the music turned up so loud that, were sound able to travel through space, the nearby ships would be lodging noise complaints. As it was, he didn't hear the announcement, even as it was being repeated.

His wing commander re-sent his usual strongly worded message demanding a prompt response, which came through on his mobile comms, finally getting his attention. He turned down the music ever so slightly and re-sent his usual report, with a few key details changed. Then he went back to his dance party.

While he had only been on the Borealis for a relatively short time, he had served on many ships like it. Upon being named acting captain and left to his own devices, he began making the ship feel more like home. It was not messy per se, but it wasn't exactly tidy either. He had a system of organization hidden beneath the apparent chaos and some of his choices, when it came to lighting and sound, went against regulations. Not that anyone was there to stop him.

He took advantage of the time he had aboard the Borealis to do all the things he normally was not allowed to. He played games. He watched movies. He studied whatever information he could get his hands on, which wasn't much. And he tinkered. He built things using the spare supplies and scraps he had snuck on board. Sometimes, when he was really bored, he would flex his technical skills by making minor modifications to the Borealis' internal systems. Which was part of why the ship was running better now than it had in years.

Dean got a rather angry-sounding reply from his wing commander, demanding a more properly written report, highlighting all the areas in which it had been obviously copied. With a sigh, Dean sat back down in the chair, not bothering to turn down the music as he started to fill out the report in earnest.

The diagnostics came in, causing his brow to furrow in confusion. What he saw did not fit with what he knew it should say. So, he started digging around, trying to figure out why, completely forgetting about the report.

Then he saw a pressure spike where there shouldn't be. He tried to correct it, but it was far too late.

Part of his engine exploded, rocketing his ship sideways through the neatly ordered lines of the Fleet.

"Mayday, mayday, mayday! The Borealis is experiencing unexpected technical difficulties! Ship needs assistance! Ship needs assistance!" he shouted into the inter-fleet radio.

To his surprise, it was not his wing commander who responded, but a voice he didn't recognize.

"Borealis, this is Prism. Please correct your trajectory. You are about to enter my lane," Grace said.

"Negative Prism, I am unable to control my ship. I repeat, I have lost all control of my ship." Even though he knew it was hopeless, Dean kept trying everything he could think of to regain some semblance of control over the Borealis. Nothing responded, though.

"Engage emergency procedures, then. You are on a crash course..." Something about the annoyance in her voice sent Dean's panic into overdrive.

"NOTHING IS RESPONDING, PRISM! PLEASE, EITHER HELP ME OR MOVE OUT OF THE WAY BEFORE ITS-"

The Borealis collided soundlessly with the Prism, knocking both ships out of the Fleet formation. Both captains were rendered unconscious on impact as the basic safety measures kicked on.

The Silver Wing Commander Kyle Jones checked the ship's names off the list as their reports came in, only giving the reports a cursory glance to ensure nothing was obviously wrong. The routine had become monotonous, but expectations needed to be met. He hoped his post remained boring until long after their arrival to Canis Orion. He had his fill of action in the skirmishes with the Empire. He felt he earned some peace and quiet.

A voice squawked over the radio, drowned out by garbled music, most definitely not a noise he was used to hearing. Something came through that sounded a bit like 'mayday' before it cut out. He checked the scanners for any signs of abnormalities, but by the time he had the correct screen pulled up, nothing showed as out of the ordinary.

Shrugging, he began drafting up a reminder that the radio is only meant to be used in case of emergency, then went back to watching his soap opera.

Grace groaned, trying to make sense of the jumble that had become her mind in the sudden, intense chaos that felt more like a nightmare than something that could possibly have been real. She must have fallen asleep again, and this time she had the most upsetting dream. Some idiot lost control of their ship and crashed into hers, sending both ships plummeting to the surface of a nearby planet. There had been a lot of screaming, a lot of swearing, and more alarms than she ever wanted to hear going off at once. Even now she could hear some of them echoing in her subconscious.

Except, no matter how hard she tried, she couldn't get the noise to stop.

Then she realized it wasn't just her imagination. The alarms were really going off, and even more unnerving, the engine had shut down.

"Wait, what? Oh no. No no no no no..." She sat up and reached for the console, frantically typing in the emergency codes, running through all the protocols she knew to make sure the Prism was okay. The ship was stable and not prone to exploding, but it was far from okay and far from flight-worthy.

"Okay, we can work with this. It's going to be okay," she muttered to herself, turning on the Fleet radio. "Mayday, mayday, mayday. This is Lieutenant Grace Dillard of the Prism. My ship was struck by an unknown object, and I crash landed on a nearby planet. Requesting emergency assistance. Repeat, ship in need of assistance."

No response.

"Repeat, this is Lieutenant Grace Dillard of the Prism. Unforeseen circumstances have caused me to crash land on a nearby planet. I am unable to rejoin the Fleet without assistance. My transponder is active. Please, can someone come assist?"

"There's no point, Dillard," an unfamiliar voice grumbled through the speaker. "These radios don't have enough signal to get through the atmosphere without some kind of booster. Plus, you were out long enough that the Fleet would be out of range anyway."

"Excuse me. Who is this? Identify yourself."

"Name's Dean. Dean Lindsay. I am currently trapped in the Borealis."

"The Borealis?"

"Yes. The Borealis. It's a med shuttle-"

"You're the idiot who lost control of his ship! You're the reason I am in this mess!"

"First off, it's not entirely my fault," Dean said defensively. "My ship was working just fine until I experienced a sudden, catastrophic failure, and I did warn you to get out of the way. Second, did you miss the part where I am trapped? I am willing to apologize for getting us both in this mess. Can you please give me a hand getting out of my ship?"

Grace huffed, slumping back into her chair. This was not part of any of her plans. She pinched her arm repeatedly, hoping the pain would be enough to wake her up.

It didn't work.

"Hey Dillard? I know this is a lot to process, but if you could please let me out of this tin can, we can get started trying to fix this situation," Dean prodded.

"One thing at a time, Lieutenant Lindsay. I must make sure it is safe for me to leave my ship before I try and help you leave yours. And will you please call me by my title? You are being incredibly unprofessional."

"Apologies, it's just getting a little toasty here in this tin can. I think the crash took out my temperature regulation and I can't fix it from the inside."

Grace didn't bother responding until she had finished doing her initial check, according to Fleet regulations. "Well, I have good news and bad news. Good news, I am not stuck in my ship. Bad news, the air on this planet isn't something we should breathe for any extended period. Do you have a suit on board?"

"That I do, and good news, it's intact. Oh, and it's a medic suit too, so it's sturdy."

"Good. Put it on. I will keep getting a lay of the land and come and rescue you shortly."

"My hero."

Grace did not dignify that with a response.

Day 0

As Grace exited her ship, wearing her surveyor's suit, she took a moment to inspect the outside before going to find the *Borealis*. The impact of the landing had caused a disturbance in the local fauna, but she was relieved to find that the ship had slid for a few yards before coming to a stop. That meant that while it had kicked up quite a lot of dirt around it, it would not be overly difficult to dig it out.

She was less pleased to find that the engines looked to be in rough shape. According to the diagnostics, many of the heat vents were clogged, and it was very likely that some components had become broken or jammed. It would take some time to restore them to working order. As for the hull itself, most of the damage was cosmetic, leaving a piece of the ship's Imperial history peeking out from the mark of the rebellion.

Grace knew all the ships in the Fleet once belonged to the Empire. She also knew that all traces of the Empire had been removed in the decade long journey to Arcadius. Those that could not be removed were covered up as part of humanity began to make a new home for themselves far outside of the Empire's grasp.

She just hadn't known that the symbol still existed on the *Prism*. Not that it mattered on a practical level.

Shaking her head, she turned her attention to the task at hand.

Finding the *Borealis* ended up being simpler than anticipated, since some of the brush that fell into the engines caught fire, sending up a stream of smoke. She climbed over the hill and saw the ship resting against some broken trees, looking much the worse for wear.

"At least it's right side up and the door is near the ground," Grace muttered to herself. At least this ship didn't bear the unremovable mark of the Empire.

Several hours of creative problem solving and shouting through the hull of the *Borealis* later, Grace managed to open the door enough to let Dean out.

"Whew, thanks. Boy am I glad I didn't crash here alone," he said, stepping out into the dull sunshine. Behind him, many of his carefully organized piles of chaos had been strewn across the floor, leaving the ship looking particularly messy as the walls flashed between different colors and the radio tried to spit out some sort of music with little success. Both of those issues had already been noted by Dean, who knew how to fix them, but they did little to help Grace's first impression of the ship or its acting captain.

"I would prefer not to have crashed at all, thank you very much," Grace snapped.

"Trust me, Dillard, it was not my intention, and I can apologize until the cows come home, but that won't do a lot to fix our current situation. Is your ship also a solo crew?"

"Yes. What does that have to do with anything?"

"Rescuing us is not going to be a priority for the Fleet, unless by any chance you happen to be carrying something super important. You were the only one who responded to my distress signal, and with the damage to my ship, it's unlikely the beacon is working. Protocol says they continue until they secure their destination before sending any rescue missions for cases like ours."

"So, you do know what the emergency protocols are. Why didn't you engage them?" What little patience Grace had for Dean was continuing to dwindle past the point it had ever been pushed before.

"I tried, but everything went very wrong very quickly and nothing worked. I believe it's called catastrophic system failure, and the only real way to deal with it is with as controlled of a descent as you can manage. I did my best given the situation and again, I am sorry I wasn't able to avoid hitting you."

"Well then, do you happen to know the emergency protocol for crash landing on an unfamiliar planet?" Grace challenged.

"As a matter of fact, I do. I had some time to kill while I waited for you to get the door open."

"And?"

"Survey your surroundings. Salvage your ship. Set up an emergency distress beacon. Wait for someone to come and pick us up. Avoid engaging with or drawing the attention of any Imperial forces and if we do, we are to pretend we know nothing of the rebellion."

"Okay. That's it, then. First things first, we take stock of our current supplies. Then we get the beacon setup. Then we start on repairs. I would like to be long gone before any Imperials have a chance to find us."

"We may also want to see if we can get the ships moved closer together," Dean suggested. "Safety in numbers and all that. In case it takes them a while to come back for us."

"Yeah. Sure. Once the beacon is up and working. Also, we need to stick together in case this planet has any dangerous wildlife."

"Of course, that way we can get eaten together!"

"Can it, Lieutenant," Grace barked.

"Easy there, Lieutenant. We are both the same rank, and we are the only ones on this planet. I don't think military hierarchy really applies here."

"We need to have some sense of order if we are going to survive this. What corps are you in?"

"Medical. Why?"

"I am in the survey corps, so outside of a medical emergency, I outrank you. That means I am in charge."

"Yes ma'am. Just give me a moment to lock up the ship without locking myself out."

Grace crossed her arms in as close of an approximation to an intimidating manner as she could manage in her spacesuit. It was not effective, but Dean wasn't about to tell her that. Not when he knew he would be spending a lot of time with this rather stringent lieutenant, waiting for a rescue that might never come. Instead, he fixed the jam in the door frame, testing to ensure he could open and close the door before closing it completely. Then he gestured for Grace to lead the way.

She turned on her heel and stalked off toward where she had left the *Prism*. Dean followed close behind, his steps clunky as he tried to get the hang of walking in an unfamiliar suit across uneven terrain. The dirt shifted in strange ways beneath their boots and the light on the blue-green grass almost looked like rippling water. A small hill broke the sightline between the two ships, though the *Borealis* had landed near the edge of a forest, toppling a few of the younger trees. Grace couldn't help but marvel at the differences in the fauna from anything she had seen before, yet some things remained so familiar, as often happened across planets. The trees were recognizable as trees, but on closer inspection, the bark formed into silvery spikes, almost like scales pointing toward the ground.

"I have to say, this is a pretty nice place to be stuck," Dean commented. "Much better than some of the other planets we passed by."

"Too bad the atmosphere mix isn't better. Not enough oxygen to balance out the carbon dioxide."

"Any chance you were on a survey ground shuttle? Because if so, you might have the equipment to create an air shield. Give us some time to get out of the suits without worrying about death."

"We can make that a tertiary priority, assuming we are here for a long period of time. No use wasting resources we might need for something else."

"Fair enough, just a thought. If you don't mind my asking, how did you end up in the survey corps?"

Grace stopped walking a few yards from the *Prism* and turned to face Dean. "Why? Don't think I have what it takes to be in the survey corps?"

"I would never dare think such a thing, especially since you literally rescued me from dying in a tin can." He held up his hands in mock-surrender. "We are going to be spending a lot of time together. Figured we might as well start getting to know each other."

"Oh. Right." She turned and continued back toward the ship. "I chose to join the survey corps after graduation. I worked hard to earn my spot too. Survey corps has the best acceptance rate to the Settlement and Exploration Board."

"Ahhh, so you've got ambitions? That's cool!"

"Yes, I do. And yourself?" Grace entered the code to open the airlock and gestured for Dean to step in first, closing the door after them.

"Why did I join the medical corps?" Dean repeated.

"Yes."

"Just made the most sense at the time. Gave me a chance to see interesting places and help people. I am more comfortable fixing things than I am fixing people, but there was a need to fill, so I stepped up to fill it. It's also hard to find a spot in the Engineering Corps, so I'll probably stick with medical for a while. I am pretty good at it. Especially emergency medicine, which could prove helpful."

"Hopefully we will not be here long enough for you to need those skills, but it is good to know we have them available. First things first, though, let's get the beacon going and make sure we have enough supplies to survive until they come for us. The pieces for my emergency beacon are in the cargo bay with the rest of my supplies."

Without waiting for a response, Grace disappeared into the bowels of the *Prism*, leaving Dean with no choice but to follow or return to his own ship. He glanced around the helm curiously, taking in the tidiness and the book tucked under one of the seats. He started to reach for it when Grace shouted for him. "Hurry it up, Lieutenant. The sooner we get the beacon running, the sooner we can get rescued."

"Yes, ma'am!" He called, nudging the book further under the seat. She grumbled something in response, but he couldn't hear it. It made him laugh, though, and that took some of the edge off his unease.

Grace seemed completely confident that the Arcadius Fleet would send someone to collect them shortly. Dean was not so sure.

But it couldn't hurt to try.

While Dean set up and tested the beacon, Grace took that time to run additional scans and send out some probes to start surveying the planet. She only hoped to be there for a few days at most, and she wanted to make the most of the time.

"So, what's the verdict, Lieutenant?" Dean asked once he finished replacing the outer casing for the ship-to-ship radio. They had shed their suits, but wore air purifying masks to remove some of the strain from the life support system until Dean could find a way to fix it.

"Not seeing any signs of large carnivores in the area. No small wildlife either, but they might have been spooked by the crash. I will check again tomorrow. Other than that, there are pockets of wooded areas in the hills surrounding our crash sites, none that appear big enough to be home to anything large. I also see signs of what could be a large body of water a few hours' walk from here. In case of an emergency, we can try to use that, though I will need to run some tests to ensure it is safe to drink or use."

"We should ration our supplies anyway, just to be on the safe side. I estimate we have enough to comfortably last for about a month.

That will give us plenty of time to find a way to purify the local water. Which, if nothing else, will give us something to keep busy while we wait."

"Excellent. I also have some educational materials downloaded locally, if you find yourself in need of content to keep you occupied," Grace offered.

"Likewise, though I just have music and movies and games. You could say I've been treating this trip like a vacation."

"There are certainly more productive ways to use your time, but I trust that you know your limits and are simply acting within them. Speaking of, I think this would be a good time for you to return to your ship and begin repairs on your radio to ensure we can stay in contact in case of emergencies. Then see about getting your beacon active. If we don't hear back by the end of tomorrow, however long that is, I want us to try and boost the signal. We don't know what kind of atmosphere this planet has."

"Of course. One way or another, we are going to figure this out, Grace. We are going to be okay."

"It's Lieutenant Dillard."

"Yes, ma'am. Apologies, ma'am."

Grace did not look up as Dean entered the airlock to don his suit and leave the ship. Her attention was focused purely on the data streaming into her console, trying to piece together a way to escape this planet as quickly as possible.

She fell asleep at her console, only to wake hours later, and staggered her way back to her quarters to sleep the rest of the night.

Day 1

Emergency Log, Lieutenant Grace Dillard

This is Lieutenant Grace Dillard of the Prism. *I crash-landed on an unknown planet along with Lieutenant Dean Lindsay of the* Borealis. *He experienced an unexpected engine malfunction that made his ship unable to fly. It is unclear whether my ship can be considered space-worthy, but I am confident that it can be repaired. We will be doing our due diligence to restore order as we wait for a signal from the Fleet. I will ensure that we are prepared to defend ourselves should the Imperials find us first.*

I have complete faith in the Arcadius Fleet, though, and I will continue doing everything in my power to further our missions.

Forever striving for the stars.

As day faded into night, Grace settled in for a solid 8 hours of rest. Sleep did not come easy, though, for the silence onboard the *Prism* made her uneasy after so many weeks of nonstop flight. She no longer had the constant thrumming of the engines to mask the sporadic noises that came from the lab equipment and sample storage. Even with the doors closed, those noises echoed a little too loud down the empty halls. She ended up playing one of her introductory science courses softly through the speaker to ease some of the tension.

It worked, and before she knew it, her alarm went off. She did not hop up quite as quickly as she normally would, being more tired and stiff than she had been since basic training. She stretched and blinked, trying to make sense of what exactly felt out of place. Then she remembered the crash.

"I was so hoping that was a dream," she groaned. "At least I've done my part. Now to keep myself occupied until the Fleet sends someone for me. Routine would do me some good."

She sat up and hit the switch to turn on the lights. They flickered briefly before resuming their normal glow, giving her enough visibility to get cleaned up and changed before heading to the helm for some morning stretches and meditations. When she went to open the shutters out of habit, she was surprised to find the sun had not yet come up.

"Huh. The nights are longer here, which means we may also have longer days. Interesting. I should make a note of that and make sure the Lieutenant is aware." She paused. "Then again, the Lieutenant may still be asleep. I can be nice today and send this as a message."

She sent the email and then went back to her usual routine. Her educational read for the week was a journal written by one of the captains who led the rebels out of the Empire and to their new home of Arcadius.

The rebellion itself had started as a dispute between two political parties that escalated to the point where it became a civil war. Things continued to go awry until the leaders managed to negotiate a ceasefire. The rebels were given a chance to leave or fall in line. Most of them chose to leave, using the generation ships originally built for expanding the Empire to house the civilians while the fighters took all of the firepower they could to provide protection, should the Empire change their mind. Those ships became the Arcadius Fleet.

Grace had been far too young to remember any of the rebellion, but she did remember some things about living on the generation ships. The rebels had gone and settled in one of the many abandoned colonies that the Empire had long since forgotten about, and things had been quiet until recently when Imperial scouts started poking around. Those had triggered the long voyage she had been on when the crash happened.

As she read, she clung fiercely to the hope that what happened had been an accident, though a small part of her worried it was something more.

Dean might have already been up had he not stayed up far too late working on small repairs around the *Borealis*, trying to figure out what it would take to get the ship flight-worthy. It was not until the light from the sun reached his face through the windows that he finally awoke, still slumped over his workbench.

Flashing on the screen inches from his face was a notification that he had an unread message from one Lieutenant Dillard. He opened the message and skimmed it, then reached for the radio.

"Good morning, Lieutenant," he said, "you are no longer the only person awake on this planet."

"It's about time. Have you assembled your beacon yet?" Grace asked, skipping past any pleasantries.

Dean signed. The pieces of the beacon laid around him, just as broken as they had been the night before when he found them near the site of the engine rupture. Even with all his experience and expertise, he knew he would not be fixing it anytime soon.

"Unfortunately, it appears my beacon was damaged in the crash, to the point of being unrepairable. If I had more equipment, maybe I could make it work, but our best bet is going to be using the parts to boost your beacon. Though we will need to plan that carefully, so we don't overload the electronics," he explained.

"How can it be broken? Did you not have it properly secured?"

"I thought I did, but it must have gotten loose when things started exploding."

Grace sighed. "Very well. We will have to make do with what we have. I should be done with my initial survey of the surrounding area within the hour. That will tell us how best to adapt our schedules to the day and night cycles here. The time will pass more quickly if we know how to adequately fill it."

"Better make the most of our time stranded here on this beautiful planet," Dean said. "Care for some company?"

"Not right now, thank you. Let's keep radio contact to a minimum, save power."

"These radios don't consume a lot of power unless they are being used for long-distance broadcasts. With the solar panels functioning at their current capacity, any energy use from the radios will be negligible."

"Good to know. I still have things that require my focus here, like finding out as much as I can about where we are so I can have information to send when we make contact with the Fleet. You may reach out if you need anything."

"Okay. I guess I will talk to you later then."

Dean stared at the radio for a few seconds, waiting for a response that never came. Then he went back to his repairs, while Grace kept working on figuring out where they had crash-landed.

The work was good. It kept her busy, kept her calm, and gave her a sense of control in an otherwise unstable situation. When she finally reached the end of what she could do in one day, she settled herself in for some study.

Meanwhile, Dean continued to tinker with his portable communication devices in the helm of the *Borealis*. Every so often he set what he was working on down to check on the nav system console. It had taken some clever, spur-of-the-moment problem solving to keep the whole system from going into an irreversible shutdown. Even so, he knew it would take more time and supplies than he had to get it fully operational again.

That didn't mean he couldn't access the historical data of where the *Borealis* had been when it crashed. It may even help him figure out what planet they landed on.

Except, the data he was seeing didn't make sense and, try as he might, he couldn't find the source of the problem. So eventually he had to admit there was no problem.

Personal Log, Dean Lindsay, first day after crash

It's official. Something is up. Either the Fleet isn't going where they say we are, or we are taking a really strange route to get there. There's always the chance that Grace and I could have encountered an anomaly, but with everything else...I'm not so sure.

There's still a lot I don't know, but I'm looking for answers. I just need to be patient and to be careful.

This is just the beginning.

Day 2

Emergency Log, Lieutenant Grace Dillard

I have had to adjust my alarms and personal scheduling to better fit the day/night cycles. Both are longer than the standard. This will require some adjustment, along with the fact that the air is not suitable to breathe. The envirosuits will help lessen the severity of the problem but it is important to still be aware of.

I plan to make a few forays into the surrounding areas to gather samples to study. I am making the most of the situation and gathering information that will prove useful to the Fleet.

Forever striving for the stars.

Grace watched in silence as the colors streaked across the sky, glinting off the swirling clouds in arrays of rainbow glitter. The dancing of the light had her so mesmerized she nearly did not notice the faint noise coming from outside. When she did, her first thought was that perhaps some local wildlife had come to investigate the new object in their home. Then she recognized the sound of engines, and her heart leapt. The Fleet had sent someone to rescue them. They would be free of this planet soon.

"Permission to land, Lieutenant Dillard?" Dean's voice echoed from the radio.

"Come again?" Grace bit back her disappointment that it was not, in fact, a rescue.

"I got the *Borealis'* engines working well enough to achieve a low hover. I can't take off, but I do have maneuvering thrusters. I recommend you stay inside while I land, but if you can find a window and be my second set of eyes, that would be helpful."

"Sure. One moment." She stood and went to the side windows, opening all the shutters until she could see the *Borealis*. "I can see you. You are clear to approach." It took some very careful maneuvering, but Dean eventually managed to settle the ship a few feet from the *Prism*.

"Alright," Dean said. "That went pretty well, I have to say. I'll need to get my maneuvering thrusters back online if we want to connect the airlocks, but for now, we can just use the purifiers to get between ships. This way if anything happens, we can reach each other faster and I don't have to deal with the strange shapes flitting around outside of my windows at night. Not that they're dangerous, they're just creepy."

"Are you certain that was a good use of energy?"

"I calculated the risk before I took it. My solar panels get more light here, so the power should be fully restored in a day or so. Plus, it's unlikely the *Borealis* is going to be space-worthy any time soon, if ever."

"That's fine. When the rescue comes, they can arrange for a tug back to the Fleet."

"I am sure they can," Dean said. "Say, do you mind if I come aboard? It feels weird talking through the radio when I can see you through the window. I promise to not be a bother, and you can kick me out at any time."

Grace considered for a moment before replying. "If you can help me adjust the life support systems to compensate, you can stay."

"Deal. Let me get my tools."

Minutes later Dean boarded the *Prism* with a bag slung over his shoulder. With Grace's supervision, he went straight for the life support system and got to work. She opened the door to the engineering bay and pulled the chair along the track so she could see through to see what Dean was doing. Then she went back to work on her course, occasionally getting up to lend Dean a hand. The course work took less time to complete than she expected, so when she finished, she pulled up one of the books she read for fun.

Dean tuned the world out as he worked, settling into the familiar rhythm that came with tinkering. The situation may have been chaotic and this strange new world they found themselves in may hold a lot of unknowns, but this was something he could fix. At the very least it would improve the quality of their life on this planet, as well as making it easier for them to get the *Prism* back in working order. Much as it pained him to admit, he knew that short of a miracle, the *Borealis* would not be leaving the planet any time soon.

"Permission to play some music, captain?" he asked after a few hours of silence. "You can pick the genre. I just need some background noise to keep my mind from wandering while I work."

"Hmmm...sure, music sounds like a good idea. I don't have the widest library, but I have a lot that have a steady beat and easy to follow lyrics that I find helpful when focusing on manual tasks. I'll get it started and put the controls on your screen."

Dean nodded his thanks and took a few seconds to scroll through the playlist before picking one of the more upbeat songs. "If you are ever interested in expanding your musical repertoire, I have amassed quite the collection and I am happy to share. I don't really do well with silence...though I promise that while we are here, I will keep my volume at a more reasonable level."

"That is appreciated, especially considering that as a medical professional you should know the dangers that loud decibels can pose to your hearing."

"Don't worry, Dillard, I always use adequate ear protection when I turn it up that high. I have no intention of blasting out my eardrums. I just sometimes like to feel the music."

"Did you spend time near the front line?"

Dean had expected her to call him out for not using her proper title. He hadn't expected that question.

"Why do you ask?" he asked.

"I was working on a battlefield psychology course the other day and they talked about how those who spent time on the lines can be uncomfortable with silence. One of the recommended options for trauma therapy and coping mechanisms is music with a loud, rhythmic bass beat. It helps remind the panic part of your brain that you are still alive."

"I guess that makes sense," Dean conceded, returning to his work. "I spent a little time near the front lines, though most of my tours were more in the backwater places. Things got messy sometimes, but I was there to try and help pick up the pieces. I've always worked better with music, though."

"Understandable. I also enjoy music while I work. Makes things feel less quiet, more normal."

"Exactly. Remind me later and I will share my library with you once I'm done adjusting your life support."

"If you don't mind my asking, what exactly are you doing?" Grace asked. Dean stepped aside to show her the screen displaying the status of the life support system.

"Since you are the only person assigned to be on this ship, they imposed artificial limits to try and conserve energy. I can't do anything about the programming but I can improve the efficiency of the system so it can handle the load of two breathing people easier, and you don't have to replace the filters as often."

"How did you learn how to do this?"

"I have done a lot of traveling and more often than not I traded work for transport," Dean explained. "Gave me a chance to see a lot of fun places and learn how to fix a lot of different ships. Plus, sometimes when I'm really bored, I flip through maintenance manuals. I can talk you through it if you want."

"My mom always said to never miss an opportunity to learn something new from an expert," Grace said meaningfully.

"Not sure I'd call myself an expert but if you're interested in learning I am happy to teach."

Grace stepped up and gestured for Dean to continue. He walked her through the steps he was taking, giving her a chance to help along the way and patiently answered all her questions.

"Perhaps after your medical tour finishes you can try getting a job teaching engineering. It might not be the same as working in the corps, but you are very good at it," Grace commented. Dean flashed a smile her way, then turned his attention back to the diagnostic he was running on the life support system.

"I have thought about it, but I need a few more tours before I can be considered for a position like that. It is on my list of possibilities though." The screen flashed and trilled. "And voila, your life support system can now safely support three people without having to override any of the Fleet regulations."

"Impressive."

"It's more time-consuming than it is challenging but having an extra set of hands made it easier."

"Well, you are welcome to stay onboard if you wish, or you can return to your ship," Grace offered. She hadn't realized how much she missed having someone else around, even though she had just met Dean.

"I think I might head back to my place and take a nap, but I may come back later if that's okay with you. It's been nice having company after traveling alone for months."

"It has been. So long as you ask first and agree to maintain professional boundaries, you are welcome aboard my ship. There will be no indulging in improper behavior, regardless of location." She tried to keep her voice even as she drew this boundary, maintaining steady eye contact with Dean in the hopes that he wouldn't be one of the men who reacted poorly to such things.

"Of course," Dean replied, not backing down from her gaze. "We need to trust each other, which means no pushing boundaries or buttons. If you don't want me to come over, I won't. I just ask that you stay in contact via the radio so I can know you are okay, and if anything needs fixing, please don't hesitate to ask. I quite literally don't have anyone else, and I would like to make sure both of us live to see the stars again," he said firmly, looking her right in the eyes. After a few seconds, her gaze softened, and she nodded.

"I promise to keep in contact. You go enjoy your nap. I am going to focus on my studying."

"Roger that, Lieutenant."

Dean put his suit back on and returned to the *Borealis*. He had a list of repairs and upgrades he wanted to make but after hours of work and more social interaction than he had had in the past months, he had just enough energy to take off the suit and plug in his oxygen filter before dropping into his cot.

When he finally awoke, he busied himself with a few of the more urgent repairs before grabbing some rations and his tablet and returning to the *Prism*. Grace allowed him on, and they sat in a mostly comfortable silence until the sun started to go down.

"I guess that is my cue to leave," Dean said. "I thank you for allowing me to keep you company."

"It's actually been kind of nice having someone else on board," Grace admitted.

"Well, if you ever need a friendly face, you know where to find me. For now, though, I bid you goodnight."

Personal log, Dean Lindsay

No new answers today. Both ships are now in a better state than they were after the crash, though, so that's something. Once I get all the emergencies dealt with, hopefully I will be able to get to some of the historical data.

At least I'm not alone. I feel terrible for saying that but having someone else here may be the only thing that keeps me from doom spiraling. She may also be my way off this planet. Or, her ship is, though I will need her help to repair it. I just wish there was something I could do to make her feel better.

I still haven't told her about where we are. I know I should, I just couldn't bring myself to do it today. I didn't want to worry her in case I was reading the data wrong. There is a chance my nav calculations are off.

I don't think I'm wrong, though.

Tomorrow. I will tell her tomorrow. And in the meantime, I'll think of something to help soften the blow.

Day 3

Emergency Log, Lieutenant Grace Dillard

There has been no change in our current situation. The beacon is transmitting, and I have attempted to calculate how long we have until we can expect a response based on the speed at which the Fleet was traveling and how long it took us to get the beacon operational, but there are too many variables for me to do so accurately. Perhaps Lieutenant Lindsay will be able to provide some assistance. He seems rather competent with technology and may know of a way to get the information we need to figure out where we are.

In the meantime, I will continue with my environmental studies and my personal education goals.

Forever striving for the stars.

Grace waited until a few hours after sunrise before she reached out to Dean via the radio. She understood the importance of rest but there was too much work to be done for her to allow him to sleep the day away.

"Good morning, Lieutenant," he mumbled groggily when he finally answered her hail. "It seems I overslept this morning. My apologies."

"Adjusting to a new day/night schedule can be difficult for anyone, Lieutenant. Give yourself a few days and you will be fine," Grace said gently.

"It would probably help if I didn't stay up all night working."

"It certainly would. Routine is important when facing difficult situations." Her mother had said the same thing to her before, and it had always proven true.

"You're right, you're right. I'll get myself sorted and be back on track by tomorrow."

"Excellent. Speaking of our situation, I have been trying to calculate approximately where we might have landed but I don't have enough variables to do so accurately. Would you perhaps be able to assist?"

"Certainly." Dean was glad she could not see the way he deflated at this. "Would you be willing to come aboard the *Borealis*? I was able to restore access to some of my historical navigational data that could be helpful."

"Oh, of course! Give me a moment and I will be right over!"

Dean cringed slightly at the enthusiasm in Grace's voice. The slow speed at which most of his computers were loading would spare him from having to immediately deliver the bad news, but there wasn't much that could soften the blow. He could only do his best to be supportive and hope Grace was as strong as he thought she was.

As he waited for her to arrive, he bustled about, trying to make the ship look a little more presentable. A few rooms were too chaotic to effectively clean in such a short period, so he decided to close those doors and focus on the main common areas instead. No need to expose her to the chaos of his creative process, unless she needed the distraction.

"This is Lieutenant Grace Dillard, requesting permission to come aboard."

He jumped as her voice crackled through the ship's intercom. "Permission granted. Just one second."

He jogged the short distance to the airlock to begin the process, making a mental note to check out the intercom system when he had the time.

A few minutes later the airlock had cycled through, and Grace was onboard the *Borealis* for the second time in her life. This time, though, she wasn't here to literally take stock of the place, so she did so metaphorically, noting some of the countless small changes Dean had made over the past few days. The piles of junk were no longer strewn across the floor and the lights were either holding steady or turned off.

"How are repairs coming along?" Grace asked politely. "I see that much of the cosmetic damage caused by the crash has been fixed."

"Yes, and I have been working on the structural issues as well. Thankfully, none of the internal integrity has been compromised. It's just going to take more time and materials than I have to properly fix everything. I've been doing whatever I can in the meantime to make it more livable, considering we don't know how long we are going to be here," he said, admiring his handiwork.

"Comfort is important, but I don't want us getting too comfortable here. That can lead to complacency and that can keep us from rejoining the Fleet."

"And the sooner we can finish our tours and go home," Dean added. "I don't know about you but this whole thing has me feeling a little homesick, especially since we have been no-contact for so long."

"Likewise, but I try to not dwell on it for too long. In the face of uncertainty, focus on what you can control. Something my mom used to say when I was stressed out at the Academy."

"Your mom sounds like a very smart woman."

"She is. Now, let's get to business. I want to start narrowing down our possible landing sites so we can pass that information onto the Fleet when we regain contact."

"Of course. Right this way." Dean held his arm out toward the helm, letting Grace take the lead. She strolled confidently into the helm and took a seat next to the navigational display, which had fallen asleep since he had last used it. "It may take a moment for me to get everything pulled up but in the meantime, feel free to make yourself at home."

"Thank you," Grace replied, settling herself into one of the seats that could rotate around to face different parts of the helm. She watched silently as Dean typed in the codes and commands to boot his systems back up and regain access to the information he wanted to access. After a few minutes of silent staring, he decided to speak.

"You've already seen some of what I do to make the ship feel more like home. I also find certain kinds of music remind me of home, especially the stuff that has a really strong beat to it. What about you? What are some things that help you beat homesickness?" he asked, letting lose his curiosity.

"It probably sounds silly, but I find a lot of comfort in routine. I like having an order and a rhythm to things. Finding order in the chaos and making steady progress on things. It helped me advance rather quickly through the Survey Corps and keep my head when things get hectic."

"I can totally understand that. It's part of why I tinker. Fixing things I can fix."

"Exactly. I also need to do a lot of work to get to where I want to be, so making consistent progress is helpful. I also have some videos I made with my mom before I left for the Academy. Little pieces of home to remind me why I am doing this. She would send me videos regularly up until we had to go dark. Lots of updates on unimportant things and videos of the cats that wander around our neighborhood," Grace said, smiling fondly, though there was a hint of sadness in her eyes, mixed with nostalgia.

"You're a cat fan?"

"Yeah. When I was little this mangy little kitten showed up at our door during a storm. Mom tried to put her foot down, but the little guy was just too sweet with those big eyes and the tiny little mews. He won her over in a matter of hours. He was my responsibility but so long as he didn't make a mess in the house, we could keep him. We grew up together until one day he got sick and all we could do was make him comfortable. We got in the habit of leaving out food for the strays after he passed, though we were both too busy to adopt one."

"That's sweet. We moved around too much to have pets, but I can definitely see the appeal. I'm sorry to hear about your cat."

"It's alright. It was a long time ago. Anyways, we have work to do. You said you were able to access the historical navigation data?"

Dean sighed. "Took some creative problem-solving, but I was able to access our earlier flight path if not our destination. With this I can glean a general trajectory of where the Fleet might be in relation to our current location with some small amount of accuracy. Once we get a pingback from the beacon, I will be able to narrow that down significantly."

"Excellent. How close are we to Canis Orion?" Grace asked, leaning forward to get a better look at the display.

"This is roughly where we were when the explosion happened," Dean pointed to the last data point he had been able to gather. "We were somewhere in the Comae Lyra system."

"And where is that in relation to the Myron asteroid belt?"

Dean hit the button to zoom out on the display until the asteroid belt in question appeared on the screen. Grace stared wordlessly at the screen, trying to wrap her mind around the absurd distance between where they should have been and where they were.

"That can't be right," she said finally.

"It is. I double-checked. The data is accurate. Wherever we were going, it wasn't Canis Orion, unless we were taking the long way."

"Well, there must be a reason we were taking that route. We were either disguising our end destination or trying to avoid the Imperials. There must be a reason."

"I am sure there is," Dean said gently, "that doesn't change the fact we are in the Comae Lyra system, far from where anyone outside of the Fleet would have expected us to be. That means if we don't manage to establish contact before they get out of range, it could be a while before they send anyone for us. I know that's scary, but it's good that we know that. Now that we know, we can plan accordingly. We are going to be okay."

"What if they don't come for us? Or what if someone else gets here first?"

"Then we will do what we need to do to keep ourselves safe. We are both smart, capable people. We may not know what is going to happen, but we can prepare to be as ready for it as we can. Just focus on what we can control, and one way or another we will find a way off this planet."

"You're right. You're right. I just...I think I need to go back to my ship and look at my defenses. I also want to finish my sweep of the area to ensure there are no hostile predators nearby." Grace straightened, tucking her emotions behind her well-practiced mask.

"Whatever you need to do. I've got some things to work on here but if you need me for anything, don't be afraid to ask."

"I won't. Thanks."

She hustled out and returned to the safety and comfort of the *Prism*, ready to bury herself in work until she could think about their situation without wanting to panic. Their situation was filled with unknowns but some of them she knew how to deal with. Having more knowledge would help them make better decisions and help her feel less hopeless.

Dean kept busy working on the *Borealis* while Grace finished up her initial survey of the surrounding area and began another. All the while, she kept a close eye on the long-distance communication systems, waiting for any sign that the Fleet responded to their beacon.

No sign came.

Then about an hour before sunset, she got a call from Dean.

"Apologies for the intrusion Lieutenant, but it seems a few of my systems need a complete reboot to start functioning properly again. I would personally prefer to not be onboard while this happens as it will become rather unpleasant in here, but I also don't want to impose on your hospitality without giving you some time to get ready to be hospitable," he said.

"How long will it take?"

"Twelve hours, give or take. I am perfectly capable of entertaining myself and perfectly content to stay out of your way. Or if you have anything else that needs fixing, I can help with that."

"Give me an hour and I will fix a space for you."

"Roger that, Lieutenant. I appreciate it."

Dean used that hour to double-check his work while Grace finished the book she was reading. She always kept the *Prism* relatively spotless, including the additional rooms, so there was little prep work that needed doing. He had said he didn't mind waiting, and she only had a few chapters left and she just had to know what happened. She finished the epilogue with a few minutes to spare, which she used to bask in the feelings the story had left her with. Then she tucked away her book, straightened her jumpsuit, and went to let Dean in.

"Thanks again for letting me come on board," he said as he removed his helmet.

"No problem. It would be ill-advised for you to be aboard your ship while everything restarts. Do you have a method of remotely monitoring your systems?"

"Yep! Everything is synched to my tablet, and I can make any necessary adjustments from here." Dean held out his tablet so she could see the information scrolling across the screen.

"Good. You are welcome to sleep in any of the other crew quarters." She pointed down the hall to where she had left the doors open. "My room is keyed to my access only, so you will not be able to enter. Anything you need you are welcome to, within reason, of course."

He gestured to the bag at his side. "I brought a project to work on, as well as some rations. I didn't want to impose."

"It's not an imposition but I appreciate it," Grace said. "I plan on eating my dinner while I watch the sunset in the helm. It's quite beautiful to watch how the colors change as the day ends."

"That sounds wonderful. In the meantime, I can check the rest of your ship to see if there's anything else I can fix or improve. I've been fixing up mine, may as well fix up yours too. With your permission of course."

"That is fine by me, under one condition. I want to watch. Maybe I can learn something new, which is always helpful."

"Since you are letting me sleep in your space, the least I can do is teach you some tricks. And if we end up needing to make our own way off this planet, I am going to need a second set of hands."

"You worry too much. The Fleet will send someone for us. We just have to be patient."

Dean let the matter drop, choosing to stick to the topics he felt more comfortable with. He fell into a comfortable rhythm working with Grace, something that brought an unexpected touch of normal. They worked off and on until it was time to eat, then watched the sunset together.

The change was subtle at first, the sky shifting from a pale blue into a much deeper shade. Then the blue mixed with a rich, royal purple and the sky above it filled with hues of orange and pink, with hints of green etched along the edges of the clouds. For the next several minutes the sky was awash with stunning jewel tones mixing and slowly but surely growing deeper and darker as the sun slowly slipped below the horizon.

"Amazing," Dean muttered as the last of the light faded from the sky.

"It really is, isn't it? If you'll excuse me, I am going to retire to my quarters. It's been a long day, and I could use some rest."

"Before you go, I made you something."

"You did?"

"Well, more accurately, I modified one of the programs we had onboard the *Borealis*. It's meant to be a sort of mental health tool, giving soldiers a companion that they have to take care of to help them through their own treatment. I adjusted some of the programming so it's a little less needy, but if you allow it to scan the videos of your cat or any of the other cats you have videos of, it can replicate their behavior. It's not quite the same as a real cat, but it's less maintenance and perfectly friendly. I thought you might like a little taste of home." He held out the small orb that would emit the projection.

Grace recognized the technology, having seen similar iterations of it before. She had honestly never considered using one to make a virtual pet. The earnest care that shone in Dean's eyes as he handed it to her nearly brought tears to her eyes.

"Thank you," she said, unable to find any other words. "Thank you."

"You're welcome. Now go get some rest. I'll see you in the morning."

She rushed back to her room and plugged the hologram machine into her console. Directing the learning algorithm was simple enough, especially since all of her cat videos already had their own individual folders from a day, she had been particularly bored. A message popped up asking which cats she wanted it to build a profile on. She selected a few of them, prioritizing her own cat over the others.

A little progress bar appeared on the screen, showing that it would take several hours to complete. With that, she flopped into her bed and finally went to sleep, dreaming of the life she left behind.

When she awoke the next morning, she found Dean asleep, curled up in the navigator's chair. She laughed and let him stay until he was awake and ready to leave.

Day 6

Emergency Log, Lieutenant Grace Dillard

Rations are holding steady. Ship repairs are continuing on schedule. Quality of life has been steadily improving over the past few days. I have spotted some signs of potentially dangerous wildlife, but they have yet to approach. I have tasked drones to keep an eye on them, in case something in their behavior pattern changes.

There have been no pingbacks from the Fleet yet. There have also been no signs of Imperials in the area.

The mental health support program Lieutenant Lindsay provided me with has greatly boosted my morale. This helps me find the energy to continue pursuing my goals and the goals of the Fleet. Though, I hope we will not be here much longer.

Forever striving for the stars.

"Good morning, Lieutenant," Dean said as he stepped into the *Prism*. He came over at least once a day to either work on something or just be in the same space as Grace for a while. He claimed it helped with his focus, but he knew they both enjoyed the reminder that they were not alone in this stressful situation, even if she hadn't admitted it.

Seeing as there were fewer things that had to be checked on regularly, being grounded versus flying in the formation, they found themselves with even more time to fill and both could only stand so much silence during the day. So, they worked together, and they talked about all manner of unimportant things, until Grace realized she had started seeing Dean as more of a friend than a colleague.

"You can call me by my last name," she commented. "Feels a little silly to keep calling each other Lieutenant at this point."

"Roger that, Dillard. It's always felt weird to have people call me by my last name, so you can just call me Dean." He turned to fiddle with something so she couldn't see the way he was absolutely beaming at this latest development. Something about watching her slowly lower some of her walls around him warmed his heart. Dean liked Grace, he couldn't help it, and he very much wanted to be her friend.

And not just because she was the only other person on the planet.

"Fair enough. Say, Dean, would you mind checking my communication system?"

He looked over to where she sat scrolling through the most recent diagnostics on one screen, with the communications log pulled up on the second screen. In the past few days, she had been spending more and more time like this.

"Still no response from the Fleet?" he asked gently.

"All attempted pingbacks have proven inconclusive. As far as I can tell there is nothing in the atmosphere that would cause any extreme interference, and I see no signs of an asteroid belt nearby. It must still be messed up from the crash."

He knew it wasn't. He also knew saying that would not help her anxiety in the slightest, so he agreed and plugged his tablet in to run yet another round of tests. They would take at least an hour to complete and while he didn't expect to find anything, he didn't mind running them again. Maybe this time he would be proved wrong.

"How is your engineering course coming along?" he asked.

"You were right about the learning curve being steep, but with your help I've managed to keep up and I am starting to wrap my head around some of the more complex concepts. Thanks again for the suggestion."

"I haven't had a chance to take it myself yet. I still have some work to do on the medical side before they will let me take any other corps' classes."

"Well, I have more than a few courses downloaded," Grace offered. She collected them whenever she could, even if she didn't have the proper qualifications to be officially pursuing such an education. "If you would like, I can recommend them to you. It won't count officially, but you can at least audit them. Then when we get back you can try for the certification."

"I will absolutely take you up on that. The days here are seriously long and reading through maintenance manuals gets a little boring after a while."

They fell into a comfortable silence as Dean kept an eye on the system check and Grace went through her collection of classes, sending him recommendations on a few she thought he might find interesting. Only one of them was an introduction to being a shuttle pilot. He laughed at that one and moved it to the top of the list.

"You said they would probably respond to our beacon when they reach the asteroid belt," Grace said as the numbers ticked down on the timer.

"That would be standard procedure in this situation."

"And how long is it supposed to take them to reach it?"

"We were about a week and a half, maybe two weeks away depending on if there were any unexpected issues."

"So, we don't need to be worried yet that they haven't responded?"

"Nope. Though if it helps, I have a few more calculations to run before I can implement my plan to boost the beacon."

"Oh good. How long do you need to finish that?"

"Give me a day and I can have it done and tested. There's no way they won't be able to hear us when they hit Jump Point Omni."

"Okay, good. We just have to keep ourselves occupied and make sure we are ready when they respond."

"Yep. Everything will be fine, Dillard." The diagnostic completed and showed all systems to be in working order. "Everything will be fine."

"It's fine. They're just following protocol. They won't forget us." She forced her face into a smile to better convince herself that she believed what she was saying. Giving into her anxieties wouldn't accomplish anything.

"They won't. We just need to keep busy. Why don't you work on one of your courses and I will finish up my calculations?" Dean suggested. He had only known her for a few days, but one thing they had in common was the need to stay busy and focus on things they could actually control.

"Yeah, that's a good idea," Grace said. She shifted her attention away from the screens and pulled out her tablet. Dean watched her out of the corner of his eye until he was certain she had become lost in the work instead of herself. Once he was satisfied, he started working on his calculations, settling into the comfort of math. It gave him something to count on in a time of chaos.

When he got tired of that, he started pursuing other thoughts that were bouncing around in the back of his mind. He needed projects. He needed to keep busy. Then he had an idea.

"Hey Dillard, you okay on your own for a bit? I have a thing I want to try, and I'd rather do it on the *Borealis* in case it doesn't work out like I think it will. I know the systems better so I can fix them easier than I would be able to yours. Also, I would feel bad if I broke your computer."

"I appreciate you not breaking my things, and I promise, I am perfectly capable of surviving without you."

"If you need anything, you know where to reach me." He gave her shoulder a gentle squeeze as he passed behind her in what he hoped came across as a reassuring gesture.

"Likewise, Dean."

He spent the rest of the day on the *Borealis*, trying to see if he could get his idea to work. As the sun crested over the horizon once more, marking the start of the seventh day, he finished. The screen showed it would take a few hours for the changes to go through, so he settled back into the seat to rest his eyes for a few minutes, and promptly fell asleep.

Personal Log, Dean Lindsay

The more I investigate what happened the more I don't like what I see. Things aren't adding up. Hopefully rebuilding the intranet connection will help give us some answers, though I have no idea what we are going to find.

What if this is my fault?

Day 8

Hey mom. Sorry I haven't written in a few days. Things have been a little hectic. Another Lieutenant and I crash landed on an unfamiliar planet a little over a week ago.

Before you worry, I want you to know that we are both okay. Neither of our ships are space-worthy but they are both secure and functional enough to keep us safe and comfortable. The planet is nice, too. I've been collecting all kinds of plant and mineral samples to study in my spare time, when I'm not working through my classes or helping Dean with maintenance. He's the person I crashed with, and he's been an absolute gentleman. I think you'd like him. He is also a whiz when it comes to tech and engineering. If there is anyone who can get me off this planet, it's him.

I've got some pictures and videos to share with you when I get home. Maybe once we are done battling the Imperials, I can take you to visit.

Oh, I forgot to mention, Dean was flying a medical ship, so we are well supplied there. He also modified one of the mental health support holos to act like Whiskers. It was really sweet of him, and it's made this ship feel a lot less lonely.

I still miss you bunches. Love you to the stars and back.
Grace

"And...perfect!" Dean exclaimed as the program began its work on Grace's computer. "It will take a few hours, but this should allow you access to the general Fleet communications and the intranet. Any queries you post will take time to load and I haven't found a way to boost our signal enough to get a full message through without it taking ages or burning out both of our ships, but it's a step in the right direction. Keep in mind, this will only show us what was on your local backup for the Fleet intranet, so it won't be the most up-to-date, but at least it's something."

"Maybe you could use the beacon?" Grace suggested.

"That is an option, but I'd have to find a way to do it without damaging the integrity of the beacon. I am looking into it, along with some other options. Hopefully getting this access to the intranet will prove helpful."

"And hopefully it won't be too much of a drain on our energy resources."

"Oh, I'm not worried about that," Dean said. "With the long days here and our proximity to the sun, we are getting enough energy stored up that we could last a month with no light and still be fine. In fact, if this keeps up, we may need to start using more energy to keep things from overheating."

"That is good to know. Shall we get to work on boosting the beacon or do we need to keep an eye on this?"

"Let's get started on the beacon before it starts to get hot outside. I have some fixes that I can run remotely if something happens."

"Very well. Let's suit up then."

Dean had much more practice putting his suit on after eight days of coming over to visit Grace, but she didn't take much longer than him. Soon they were taking the pieces of his partially repaired beacon out to hers, along with a selection of tools.

"Have to say, I am glad gravity is almost the same strength here as it is back on Arcadius," Dean commented. "This would be a little more complicated otherwise."

"Are you sure you properly factored that into your calculations?" Grace asked nervously.

"Yes. I double-checked your math and then triple-checked mine. I am as certain as I can be, and I erred on the side of this being a waste of time as opposed to messing up the beacon."

"Okay, good. I trust you. Let's do this."

They spent the next few hours carefully piecing together the beacon booster. Dean explained his thought process with each step and got Grace's help to test its efficiency. She asked good questions too, and between the two of them they were able to fashion a rather effective booster for the emergency beacon.

"You are really good at this," Grace commented.

"Fixing things is my passion."

"Not just that but finding clever solutions and explaining them to people. For what it's worth, when we get back to the Fleet, I am more than happy to vouch for your skills."

"I appreciate it. I also think we need to do this more often. Not the beacon boosting but spending time outside. I didn't realize until recently just how cooped up we've been."

"Well, we have had a very good reason for doing so. The air here could kill us if we breathe it too long and it's not like we could have gone for a walk while we were traveling with the Fleet."

"Yes, but now we are stuck planetside, and we have these lovely suits that let us breathe healthier air for hours at a time. Maybe we can't do a day hike, but we can go for a walk about every day or so, stretching our legs. It'll be good for our sanity, and for our physical health."

"Hmmm...you make a good point. So long as we are smart about it, I don't see the harm," Grace admitted.

"Yes!" Dean exclaimed. "Would you care to join me for a walk?"

"Hmmm...I want to check on the update, see if we can access any of the intranet communications."

"Good point. Tomorrow, then?"

"Tomorrow."

They returned to the *Prism* and Grace all but sprinted over to the console to check on the update. She let out a squeal of delight as the screen lit up with the emblem for the Arcadius Fleet. Then a message popped up saying an update was required to access the intranet. She glanced at Dean briefly as if asking permission, and he nodded. She hit the button. The screen flickered a few times before switching to a loading bar.

"Thirteen hours?" Grace exclaimed. She slumped back into her seat, sighing heavily.

"Yeah, I had a feeling that might happen. It's been out of sync for several days and the system was due an update about four days ago. According to these readings everything is working as it should. It is just going to take longer."

"I guess we better find something else to do in the meantime."

"We could watch a movie."

She perked up immediately. "You have movies?"

"I have an extensive collection of movies and shows. I even have some cartoons. And I am realizing I should have mentioned this earlier."

"Yes, you should have. I haven't seen a good movie in ages. Show me this library of yours."

"Maybe later. I don't want to overtax your systems. Thankfully, I've already got the best series ever on my local tablet, which I can hook up to a bigger screen with no issues." He tilted his tablet so she could see the screen.

"I haven't seen that one," she said.

"That settles it. It's time for a marathon." Dean started to set up the movie using one of the displays in the common area, but Grace stopped him. His heart sank, and he worried that he had crossed some invisible line.

"I know a better place. Follow me." She led him to what would have either been the captain's quarters or some sort of meeting space. It had probably been designed to serve either purpose, so as to make the most use of the space. "You can connect your tablet to that wall, and it will project however large you want it. I will take care of the seating."

"Perfect. Now all we need are some movie snacks." He found the cord and connected his tablet, pulling up the first movie in the series and adjusting the projection size. Grace's enthusiastic interest in having a movie night with Dean made him happier than he expected. Sure, he got along with his colleagues in the Fleet, but this was the first time in a long time that he felt like he had a friend.

Meanwhile, Grace grabbed onto some handles he hadn't noticed before and pulled, revealing drop down seating that looked far more comfortable than he expected. It was also, to his relief, more of a couch setup than a bed setup. Yes, he liked Grace, but he wasn't exactly looking to move that quickly, especially since they were literally the only two people on the planet.

"This ship was designed to double as an educational vessel," she explained at his curious look. "As for the snacks...I suppose the owner wouldn't mind if we broke into his stash, considering the situation. So long as we don't eat all of it."

"This ship has a candy stash?"

"Among other things, and no I will not tell you where they are. We may be stranded but we are not going to abuse the hospitality of someone who isn't here."

"By all means, keep your secrets. Just wish the *Borealis* had something exciting like that," Dean scoffed. "All I've managed to find is a few lost socks and more loose wrappers than I want to think about."

"What kind of wrappers?"

"You don't want to know. Anyways, I've just about got the movie set up. Why don't you go and grab those snacks?"

Grace ducked out of the room while Dean continued adjusting the screen settings. She had pulled down two sections of the couch with a table between them. He took the one nearest to the tablet hookup so she would not have to worry about tripping on the cord.

"You know the wall display is wireless enabled," Grace commented.

"Of that I have no doubt. My tablet, however, can be finicky when it comes to streaming media from it to another place. It works perfectly for remote monitoring, but things like this I'd rather keep it plugged in than have to fight with it."

"I trust that you know your stuff." She shrugged, then held up two bags of candy. "Fruity or chocolate?"

"Fruity."

She tossed him the more colorful bag and curled up onto the open section of sofa. Whether she had intended to or not, they did end up watching the entire series. Afterwards, she asked Dean to play the director's commentary, during which she fell asleep.

She awoke hours later to a mostly tidy, dark room, with an unfamiliar jacket draped over her like a blanket. When she went to go and find Dean, she found him once again in the helm, asleep in the navigator's seat. Instead of waking him, she draped the jacket over him and set a bottle of water near his feet. Then she returned to her quarters, locking the door behind her.

Personal Log, Dean Lindsay

This planet is starting to grow on me. Not that I'd want to live here full-time. Too many strange things going bump in the night. Apparently, most of the wildlife here is nocturnal. We haven't had any issues yet, but I am hoping we can leave before that changes.

I'd like to come back here, though, when I'm more prepared to explore properly. It's an interesting place. First things first, we need to get off this rock.

Day 11

Emergency Log, Lieutenant Grace Dillard

This has been going on longer than I expected, and still we have heard nothing back from the Fleet. We have also seen no signs of Imperial scouts, which is a relief. Every day I wake and wonder if this will be the day that changes. The only things I know about the original rebellion, back on Caelestis, were passed down to me by my mother, who wasn't directly involved. That is more than enough to make me afraid of what will happen if they catch us.

I try not to dwell on such things, of course, because it's not productive to stew in worry. I am remaining wary, though. The longer we are stuck here, the more I begin to worry that this may not have been an accident so much as it was Imperial in origin.

After the movie night, Dean returned to the *Borealis*. Twenty minutes later, it began to rain and did not let up for two days. He spent most of the first day trying to boost the radio signal so they could better communicate while Grace continued to work through two more classes to keep herself from getting bored. The second day was devoted to working on some weather prediction tech so they could, at the very least, get a forewarning when a storm was coming. Grace already had the equipment, and with Dean's help she was able to modify it. All that was left as the eleventh day began, was to deploy it.

"Time to suit up then!" Dean declared.

"Why would we need to suit up? I can handle the deployment from here."

"Yes, you can, but I for one would love an excuse to walk around outside while the weather is nice. I am starting to get a little cabin fever after being stuck in my tin can for two days."

"A short walk does sound like a good idea," Grace admitted. "We just need to be careful. No telling what this weather has done to the terrain."

"Deal. Now suit up and meet me outside in ten minutes."

"Easy there, Lieutenant. Remember who is in charge here," she chided playfully.

"Since mental health is a large part of why I want to go for a walk, I think we are both in charge."

She sighed and shook her head. "Whatever. I'll meet you outside, Dean."

Bits of his laugh filtered through the radio, bringing a smile to her face as she slid her helmet on.

The brilliant sunlight streaming through the cloudless sky left them stunned for a few seconds as their eyes adjusted to the sudden influx of daylight. As the shock wore off their shoulders started to relax.

"You were right. We need to do this more often," Grace muttered. Dean gestured for her to lead the way as they started their walk, careful not to lose his hold on the sensors. She firmly gripped the drone that would be delivering them to their destinations in both hands.

"Why don't we make a plan? We suit up and go for a walk every two to three days, for at least fifteen minutes. If we need to do a longer walk, we plan ahead accordingly."

"I think that sounds like a wonderful idea, though I don't think we will be here a whole lot longer."

"Dad taught me how to hope for the best even as you prepare for the worst, because so often things change and the cards will fall out of your hands."

"That is...really wise, if a bit convoluted. Did your dad play cards?"

"Mostly low stakes with his friends. It was a little too social to call him a gambler. He and mom owned a private shuttle business, catering to business owners and executives. It kept us pretty comfortable."

"I notice you're using a lot of past tense. Did something happen?"

"There was an accident. Mom didn't make it. Dad barely did, only to get sick a year or so later." Even though it had been years, Dean still could not keep the sadness from his voice. He missed them terribly.

"When was this?"

"Before I joined the Academy. Another family took me in so I could have a place to call home, but I always felt like more of a guest there than family. They help me out when I need it, but I mostly take care of myself."

"I am glad to hear you didn't have to go through all of that totally alone," Grace said, giving him a soft smile.

"Yeah, having people helped. What about you, though?" Dean asked. "Do you have anyone waiting for you back home?"

"It's just me and my mom. She worked a lot of different jobs when I was growing up, but she's an artist now. Nothing famous but she makes enough to take care of herself. I have part of my salary set to go into an account we share in case she ever needs anything and I'm not there to help."

"The two of you must be pretty close."

"Yeah, you could say that. She's the one who taught me how to be ambitious. She taught me the value of working hard and the importance of standing up not only for yourself, but for others. I wouldn't be the woman I am today without her. I certainly wouldn't have had the courage to join the Fleet without knowing that she would always have my back."

"She sounds amazing."

"She is. I send her messages at least once a week, letting her know how I'm doing and asking how her business is. I know I won't get to hear any of her responses until we reach our destination, but it helps when I am feeling a little homesick."

"Something to look forward to," Dean said, flashing her a smile.

"Yeah."

"Is it just me or is everything brighter here? I'm not just talking about the light, but the colors."

"I've noticed it too." Grace accepted the change in conversation eagerly. "I have been wanting to grab some more samples to run tests on, see what I can figure out about the biology here."

"Why don't we grab some on the way back? Each trip we can grab some more, building up your surveying repertoire."

"That is an excellent idea."

Neither knew what to say next, so they fell into a comfortable silence as Dean watched Grace deploy the drone. Critters chirped and cooed in the distance as the breeze rustled some of the nearby foliage. Dean found himself wondering what it would be like to truly call the planet home. Grace's mind wandered between thinking of her work and thinking of her mother. She decided then that she would take extra samples of the flower petals, as well as plenty of pictures to send back home.

By the time they had all the tech in place, clouds had begun to gather on the horizon.

"We should probably head back," Grace said reluctantly.

"Sounds like a good idea. I'd rather not be caught outside in one of these storms."

"Would you mind staying on the *Prism* tonight? I'd rather not be stuck on my own if the storm lasts for days again."

"Of course. Just let me grab some things from the *Borealis* so I don't put a dent in your supplies."

"Thank you, Dean."

"Any time, Dillard."

Unfortunately, the next storm came quicker than either of them expected, and Dean was once again stuck on the *Borealis*. This time, the rain lasted three days before it let up enough for them to venture outside.

Dean spent most of his time tinkering and working through the classes Grace had sent his way. The first few he passed with ease, happy to discover he already knew far more than he thought he did, even if he was unfamiliar with the jargon. Grace worked on her classes too, as well as exploring what parts of the Fleet intranet she could access. The loading time was slow, but she was nothing if not patient.

First, she checked to see if there was any talk of the crash. Then she investigated Dean, curious to learn more about his background and see what kind of commendations he would need to join the engineering corps.

In her search, she stumbled upon his military record and the notes left by those he had served under. Some of the things they said did not fit with what Dean had told her, so she kept digging. The more she looked, the more things didn't line up and the more questions she had. Yet the storm had grown so intense she knew any attempts to ask him would be fruitless.

So, she decided to ask him during a lull, trusting that he would be able to explain himself. Explain the discrepancies in the stories and the fact he had left such an important detail out as the family name that got him into the Fleet in the first place. The more she thought, the more she stewed, the more annoyed she became as different possible versions of the conversation played out in her head, growing closer and closer to a confrontation.

By the time the storm let up enough for her to leave the *Prism*, she was ready to blow.

Personal Log, Dean Lindsay

Note to self: when visiting this planet, make sure it's not during the rainy season. This ship isn't small, but it's still starting to feel a little claustrophobic. Doesn't help that I'm having a hard time keeping in contact with Grace. I'm sure she's fine. She always is. But I miss talking to her. She helps this place feel less lonely.

Maybe I need a holo-cat.

Day 15

I would like to lodge a formal complaint against Lieutenant Dean for dangerous misrepresentation. Not only has he been lying to me, but I think he's been lying to everyone. I don't know what kind of game he's playing but one way or another, I am going to find out. I can't believe I trusted him. I won't be making that mistake again.

Dean was more than a little confused when he opened the door to the *Borealis* to find himself facing an angry-looking Grace. Her eyes flashed with a rage that he could not begin to explain, even as he wracked his brain for what he could possibly have done to anger her so.

"Is everything alright, Grace?" he asked, not sure what else to say.

"When were you going to tell me the truth?" she demanded.

"The truth about what?"

"The crash. It wasn't an accident, was it? I saw your record, Dean. I know why you were removed from the military corp. I know you were under investigation for technical misconduct and that investigation was quashed by the Aemaris family because you are their ward. What would that investigation have uncovered, I wonder?"

"Are you trying to insinuate that I'm an Imperial loyalist?" Dean was torn between genuine concern for Grace's mental state and absolute befuddlement. Something tugged at the back of his mind, but he couldn't put his finger on it.

"I don't know, are you? You certainly have the technical know-how to sabotage your ship. Maybe you were hoping for a chain reaction? Or maybe you were the target? I don't know. All I know is that you lied to me."

"Yes, I am a ward of the Aemaris family. They took me in when my parents died. I didn't exactly have a say in it. They only quashed the investigation to save themselves from embarrassment. They never outright said it, but they still made it clear that if I wanted their support, I had to be a soldier. I had to serve in the Fleet. I never intended to stay beyond my first tour, just long enough to find another way to take care of myself," Dean retorted. Thoughts raced around his mind as he tried to untangle his feelings about this unexpected fight, but the only thing he could name for sure was guilt. Grace's eyes flared with anger.

"For someone who says they didn't want to be an Aemaris, you sure aren't afraid to use it to your advantage," she spat back.

"That was Lucas who called in the favor with the family. I was prepared to figure out my own way when the transfer orders came through. If it had been anyone else, I would have turned it down. He was the only one who didn't treat me like a lesser being. Decided to stick out the rotation for him, then got stuck when the voyage started."

"Okay, so that explains why you are still here. It doesn't explain your reluctance to fight, though. The Empire will stop at nothing to destroy the rebellion. That is why we were on the voyage in the first place, to make sure they can't find Arcadius. You would understand that if you weren't such a coward. At first, I just thought you joined the Fleet for money, but now I wonder if you've ever made a tough choice in your life. You may not have had it easy growing up but since you moved in with the Aemaris family, everything has been handed to you on a silver platter."

"Yes, everything has been handed to me but every single thing they gave me came with a price. You don't get it because you have a good mom, but since I moved in with them my life has been a nonstop dance of trying to keep my soul without earning their wrath. So long as I have to rely on them, I cannot escape their expectations, and it is going to take a hell of a lot of hard work for me to be free of them. Sure, I roll over for them and do as they say, because sometimes that's what you have to do to survive."

"Make whatever excuse you want, whatever helps you sleep at night. That doesn't change the fact that you're a coward and I don't want to see you on my ship again. I will work with you to get off this planet, but I don't know if I can trust you anymore," Grace said. She turned to storm off.

"Grace, wait..."

"It's Lieutenant."

The words caught in Dean's throat and before he could drag them out, Grace was gone. Then he realized the pounding in his head was more than just emotional turmoil. He had no suit on, no air purifier.

He slammed the door shut and stumbled back to one of the medical bays to hook himself up to the oxygen tank. The automated system informed him he was suffering from carbon dioxide poisoning. He showed all of the signs, difficulty breathing, irregular heartbeat, impaired consciousness. The protocol kicked in before he could protest, not that he had the strength too.

As he slept and his body recovered, he dreamed of Grace. He dreamed that he had chased after her to try and once again explain himself, to find some way to earn her forgiveness.

Meanwhile, Grace decided that she needed to go for a walk to clear her head. The fight had only worsened the headache she had been developing over the past day or so, and the mix of hurt and anger and confusion were certainly not helping. She just needed to stretch her legs and clear her head before getting back onto the ship.

Thunder rumbled in the distance, but she ignored it. It wasn't close. She had time.

She wandered down a vaguely familiar path, boots squelching in the mud as she had to pause periodically to wipe the moisture off her visor.

The wind buffeted Grace as she walked, causing her to stumble and nearly fall as her feet tried to tangle themselves with some of the slender, purple vines that carpeted some of the ground. They were stronger than she expected, so she took a moment to trim some and tuck them into her suit pocket to study for later. Or, she tried to. The wind tore the samples from her hands before she could get them near her pockets, and she nearly face planted trying to chase after them.

Grace stumbled around for a little longer, losing track of where she was and briefly forgetting what she was doing.

She shook her head, trying to clear it as a small part of her realized something wasn't right. She was being irrational. She needed to get back to the *Prism*. She couldn't think through the pounding in her head. When the sky broke open and the rain started to come down, she found her vision not affected as much as it should have been.

The rain also seemed to be having an effect of some sort on the exterior of her suit. That couldn't be good. Or real. She wasn't sure if it was either, but she did need to sit down until her head stopped swimming.

She tried in vain to find her way back to the *Prism* but that required too much thinking and coordination, so she settled for curling up under a big rock. She took her helmet off long enough to put her emergency breather in before closing it back up. The breather helped clear her mind some, but her head hurt so bad.

Grace called out to Dean using the suit's radio, asking for help, but he never responded. And soon, she fell into an uneasy sleep.

Day 16

Dean woke to thunder and lightning and rain. The clock informed him that he had only been unconscious for an hour and a half. The message next to the clock said his vitals were now within acceptable parameters, but the protocols recommended that he avoid any strenuous activity for the next twenty-four hours.

"Yeah, yeah, I know what I'm doing." He swiped the warning away and finished detaching himself from the medical equipment. As he did so, he tried not to think about his fight with Grace. Yet try as he might, he could not push her words from his mind. He didn't know she was capable of the rage she displayed, the venom with which she flung her accusations.

Dean busied himself with things he knew he could fix as the rain continued to pound against the hull of the *Borealis*. Hours passed as he tinkered, leaving his music running in the background to dull some of the silence. Every few minutes he glanced up at the window facing the *Prism*, not that he could see much through the water and the fog.

He paused long enough to eat half a ration pack, choosing to save the rest for dinner. They were not quite at the point where they needed to start reducing their rations, but he found he didn't quite have the appetite to eat more than that.

When the storm finally started to fade, Dean stood, stretched, and went over to the radio.

"This is Lieutenant Lindsay for Lieutenant Dillard," he said. "Come in Lieutenant Dillard."

No response came. He adjusted a few dials and tried again.

"Lieutenant, I know you are upset with me, and I completely deserve it. I just need to know if you made it back to your ship alright, and then I will leave you alone. I promise."

Still no response. He tried one of the signals he had shared with her during the first round of storms, a simple pattern to convey status.

No squawks came through from the *Prism*, only static.

He swore softly. He had to know for sure that she made it back to her ship before the storm hit. He had to know that she was okay.

So, he suited up and braced himself to head out into the deluge. Thankfully, by the time he made it outside the storm had lightened somewhat, but he had a feeling this reprieve wouldn't last. He jogged over to the *Prism* and buzzed the intercom.

"Lieutenant, it's Dean. I am here to apologize and request some sort of confirmation that you are onboard and okay. I know you don't want to talk to me, and I won't make you. Just give me some signal that you are okay, and I will leave you alone."

Again, there was no response. Nerves started to boil in the pit of his stomach. He flashed back to her anger, her paranoia, the unsteadiness of her breathing. Add to that her fatigue and constant low-level headache that she only occasionally complained about, and it painted a worrying picture. Dean plugged his tablet into the door and hacked into the security logs to see all the times the airlock was opened and closed.

She had opened it to go yell at him hours ago. It had not been opened since. Wherever she was, it wasn't on the *Prism* or the *Borealis*, and that chilled him to his core.

Dean looked at the darkness gathering on the horizon. "Where did you go, Grace?"

Even though he didn't have an answer, he knew he had to find it, and soon. The last thing he wanted was to lose the one person in his life he actually cared about, especially not while she was still angry at him.

He took a deep breath and mentally reviewed everything he had learned about tracking in his military training. He also reviewed everything he knew about Grace.

"She'd have gone somewhere familiar...somewhere safe. Think, Dean, think. Where would she have gone to hide from the storm...and from you..." His mind flashed back to one of their walks when she had been talking to him about the requirements for placing a settlement. He had kept asking her questions and at one point she called out a rock structure as being a good means of defense against the elements. She had said something about either making a cave or there being a cave that could be used for storage.

If she had been caught out in the elements, she would have sought shelter there. Assuming she had been able to find it.

He ducked back into the *Borealis* to grab his emergency medical kit, hoping to any entity that might be listening that he wouldn't need it. Then he headed out in the direction he had seen Grace leaving, activating the search signal in his suit. All medic suits had one to use in case of emergency, to help with locating anyone who was injured and unable to respond. Yet another thing he had hoped to never use, but that he was incredibly grateful to have.

He fixed the spot she showed him in his head and set off at a brisk pace, praying to all the stars that he would be able to get her back in time before the next round of storms hit. The wet ground suctioned to his boots, slowing his steps just enough to be annoying. As he walked, he kept an eye out for any sign of Grace. If she had left a trail, it had long since been washed away by the wind and the rain.

"Grace! Can you hear me? Grace?"

The wind picked up, snatching away any response, and he started to panic. He was running out of time. The storm would start again soon. He had to find her.

Dean nearly jumped out of his skin when something beeped in his ear. The connection was faint, but he was getting close.

Thunder rumbled behind him, and he started to feel his heart pounding in his ears.

He paced around in a circle until he found where the signal was the strongest, then he headed that way, trying to keep track of where he was in relation to the ships. The mud continued to hamper his progress, but he kept going, trying to place his feet on firmer ground. He had to get to Grace. He had to find her.

"Grace? It's Dean. If you can hear my voice, call out," he tried again. No response, but the ping continued to get louder, so he kept going, looking for any signs of where she could be.

All he could see was mud and roots and rock, covered in debris strewn about by the rising winds. He continued calling her name, trying to push back against the panic creeping up from the pit of his stomach.

A flash of orange caught his eye, something poking out from under a rock, only partially obscured by muck. Dean ran towards it, feeling a sliver of relief as the ping morphed into a single, solid tone.

He had found Grace. She lay, unconscious, partially covered in mud and mostly tucked under a rock outcropping, with one hand reaching out.

Dean dropped to his knees next to her, setting his bag on top of the rock as he instinctively grabbed her outstretched hand.

"It's okay, Grace," he said, squeezing her hand. "I'm here. You are going to be okay. You have to be okay."

Grace stirred slightly but didn't wake as he carefully lifted her by the shoulders and rested her against his legs so he could remove her helmet long enough to swap out her breather out for one that was medical grade, that could breathe for her. He relaxed slightly as her chest began to rise and fall more evenly. The machine would help her keep breathing for the next several hours.

Next, he slipped on the vitals monitor to see if there was anything else that needed immediate attention. Her vitals were not great, but the breather seemed to be helping. He put her helmet back in place and started wiping the mud from her suit where she had become partially buried.

Then the rain began to fall, and he realized he needed a new plan.

"Hang in there, Grace. We are going to have to stay here a little longer until the storm passes. We can weather this together, then we can get back to the ship," Dean said, grabbing his medical pack. He gently slipped it between himself and Grace, positioning it so he could reach inside should he need anything. Then he positioned himself so his body would protect Grace from the elements as the storm picked up once more.

He managed to get an emergency IV in through one of the ports on the suit, as well as a suit warmer before the sky broke open once more. Then all he could do was wait and pray that Grace would be okay.

The minutes stretched into hours stretched into what felt like days as the rain beat down on Dean and the wind sent debris hurtling into his back. Nothing punctured his suit, thankfully, but he knew he would be bearing the bruises for a while. He didn't move, though. He didn't leave Grace.

Instead, he talked to her. He told her stories he heard while growing up, stories from his own life, stories from shows he had not thought to bring with him on the journey. By the time the rain started to slow, and the wind died down, Dean had resorted to making up stories, which were not quite as good as the stories others had made, but he was doing his best to keep Grace conscious. Her vitals had been slowly improving as the storm raged, but he would not rest until she was safe on the ship.

When the rain dwindled to a gentle sprinkle, Dean took that as his cue to get moving. He extracted himself first, putting the pack back on top of the rock so he could use both hands to move some of the mud off Grace. Once he was confident she wouldn't be suctioned to the ground, he moved over to her shoulders and grabbed them, slowly but steadily moving her out from under the rock.

This movement finally caused Grace to wake just enough to be aware that she was awake.

"Dean?" she muttered.

"It's okay. I'm here now. Can you tell me where it hurts?"

"Head...arm..."

"What about your legs? Do you think you can walk?"

"Maybe?"

"Okay, good. I am going to help you up and we are going to move very slowly, okay? You let me know if something hurts, okay?"

"Okay."

Dean managed to get Grace onto her feet before the wind picked up again. She wobbled, unsteady on her feet, so he carefully wrapped her arm over his shoulder, giving her something to lean on. The suits didn't make this operation easy, but he managed it. A small ember of hope began to burn in his chest, relieving some of the fear that had been eating at the back of his mind from the moment he realized she was missing.

"There we go," he said. "How does that feel? Do you think you can walk with me, Grace?"

"Yeah, I think so," she muttered. Her head was starting to droop, so he jostled her gently. She groaned in protest.

"Come on Grace, don't you go falling asleep on me now."

"Mmmmm...tired."

"I know you're tired, Grace. That's why we are going back to the ship, okay? Let's get you inside where it's nice and warm and dry. Then you can sleep."

"Okay. Lesss go."

Her speech was slurred but her attempts at walking had a little more effort behind them, letting Dean increase the speed slightly. The rain caught up with them, but he managed to get her onto the *Borealis* before the deluge began in earnest. Then came the challenge of getting them both out of their suits and getting Grace into the medical bay before she lost consciousness.

"Easy there, Grace," Dean muttered. "I need you to stay awake a little longer, okay? Just a little longer so I can make sure you're okay."

She mumbled something, fighting to keep her eyes open as he hooked her up to the IV and a series of monitors. The whole time he kept muttering a stream of encouragement, assuring her that she would be okay. Begging her to be okay.

For the first time in his life, Dean found himself incredibly grateful for his months of required medical training. He'd have been a complete mess otherwise.

As it was, he couldn't bring himself to sleep that night. Instead, he sat up, keeping an eye on Grace. He monitored her vitals. He talked to her. He read to her. And he waited for her to wake up.

The first few days she had roused long enough to be vaguely confused and fuss at Dean for looking tired and not taking care of himself. He explained what happened, and she insisted she would be fine if he slept for a few hours.

"Why do you introduce yourself as Lindsay when your file says Aemaris?" she asked in one of her more coherent moments.

"Just because I live with them doesn't mean I'm one of them. I was born a Lindsay, and I chose to stay a Lindsay, until someone gives me a really good reason not to."

"Okay...makes sense..." She drifted back off to sleep.

He still didn't leave her side. And he did not forgive himself.

Personal log, Dean Lindsay

I almost lost Grace today. She could have died, and all because I didn't tell her the truth. I can make up all the excuses in the world but at the end of the day, she deserves better than that.

I have to make it up to her. I have to make sure she gets home. From now on, I will be honest with her. No more hiding. No more letting her pay for my stupidity. She deserves better and I am not leaving this place without her.

Day 18

Personal log, Grace Dillard

The past few days have been surreal. I still don't know how I managed to get myself in that situation, but I am glad Dean had his head on straight. I could very well have died out there.

I may not know what's going on, but I know he didn't deserve me shouting at him. Me doubting him. Me insulting him.

I owe him a chance to explain himself. And maybe an apology, if he has a good explanation.

On the 18th day, Grace's vitals finally hit the point where the machines Dean hooked her up to would allow her to be unhooked. By then she was beyond ready to be up and about, at least in her mind. Her body did not share the enthusiasm, as evidenced by her nearly falling onto the floor while trying to stand. Dean caught her just in time.

"Take it easy there, Lieutenant," Dean said, holding onto her arms until she was seated safely in the bed once more. "You have got to take it slow until you have your strength back. This is the one area in which I am an expert, remember."

"I know, I know. I am just so bored of sitting around." Grace's mother had always said she made for a terrible patient, and Dean had been getting a healthy dose of this reality since she woke up. He had remained unerringly patient, though, to her surprise.

"You haven't just been sitting around. You have been in and out of a medically induced coma for the past two days, recovering from a concussion and hypothermia."

"I am very aware of that, thanks," she grumbled, trying a second time to stand on her own. This time went much more smoothly.

"There, see." Dean's voice rang with pride and a tinge of relief. "Patience pays off. You only have to deal with me for a few more hours, then you can go back to your ship."

"That eager to get rid of me, eh?" Grace laughed. "I'm not that bad of a patient."

Dean carefully guided her through the halls, staying close enough to grab her if she fell but giving her the space she needed to move on her own. "Not at all. You are welcome to stay as long as you like. I just didn't want you to feel like you have to."

She slowly slid into one of the seats in the helm, letting out a contented sigh as she stared out the window in the slightly sunny sky. He had no idea if there would be another string of storms, but he certainly hoped the break would last. They could both use the sunshine.

"I wouldn't mind sticking around for a bit," Grace admitted. "I am still feeling a little wobbly...and I think we need to have a conversation after that fight."

"Well, if we are going to talk about that, let me go first. I am sorry that I didn't tell you. I could make up all sorts of reasons for hiding it from you but at the end of the day, you're right, I am a bit of a coward. I didn't tell you because I didn't want you to see me like that and it only proved that it was true. I'm also an idiot who sat there breathing carbon dioxide for so long that the med bay had to put me under for an hour to deal with the damage."

"Dean, I am so sorry. I shouldn't have yelled at you like that. Yes, I was angry, but I let that anger get the best of me and I didn't even think about what I was exposing you to. I am so sorry."

"It's okay, Lieutenant. You had every right to be angry at me-"

"My anger does not excuse my behavior. The way I approached that conversation was unacceptable."

"You have been in an incredibly stressful situation in an unfamiliar place, and you were showing signs of carbon dioxide poisoning," Dean explained. "I checked your suit and there was a rupture in the air supply. It was small, so easy to miss, but when you suited up and stood in the airlock you would have started feeling anxious, and the anger you already felt would have been intensified. I am not trying to dismiss your feelings, you had every right to be angry, but the lack of oxygen would have amplified that and muddled your thinking when you left."

"A rupture? Are you sure?"

"Yes. I found it when I checked your suit, after I got you stable. You weren't doing well when I found you, so I checked, and you showed signs of oxygen deprivation. That's part of why it took you so long to recover. You'll be okay, though. Most of your symptoms are gone."

"That's not possible. I triple-check my suit every time I put it on. There were no ruptures."

"Perhaps it sustained the damage when you fell."

"That would make sense…can you tell how long I was deprived?"

Dean's brow furrowed. "I should be able to, just give me a minute."

Grace leaned her head back, closing her eyes and trying one of her breathing exercises to try and center herself. Even though she was feeling considerably better than she had when she first awoke in the med bay, she had not yet hit what she would call 100%. The months of training she went through before joining the Fleet had prepared her for many things, but not the fatigue she felt now. Who knew near death experiences could be so tiring?

She could still see the flashes of light and hear the roaring of wind and rain whenever she let her mind wander too far. It almost felt unreal what she had gone through. There was still much for her to reconcile from the past few days and all of this new information was not helping with the mental fog. The more answers she had, though, the easier it would be to put the pieces together and soothe her anxiety.

So, she waited patiently for Dean to respond.

"Huh," Dean said finally. "That's odd."

"What's odd?" Grace straightened, shifting to face Dean.

"According to this, you have been suffering from long-term CO_2 exposure. I see no signs of permanent damage, so it must have been low level, but it got worse around the time of our fight. I am unsure what could have caused it, but I think I'm going to have to insist you stay on the *Borealis* until I find the source of this problem. I ran a very thorough check of the air quality and life support system here and found no issues, so we should be safe."

"Maybe something got messed up in the crash and we missed it."

"Maybe." Dean glanced up at Grace. "Come on now, Lieutenant. Don't you go falling asleep on me just yet."

"Hmm...no, I'm awake. I'm awake." Grace shifted into something more resembling an upright position. "I was just resting my eyes for a second. I've been through a lot in the past few days."

"You certainly have. Do you want to talk about it? I know the last attempt didn't go very well but I promise I am ready to answer any questions you have."

"Why didn't you tell me?" she asked, forcing the words out before she could reconsider. She deserved to know and dancing around the truth wouldn't help anyone.

"Because I don't tell anyone if I can avoid it. That name carries a lot of weight and people always treat me differently after they hear about that connection. They either butter me up to try and get in good with the family or they look at me like I've had everything in life handed to me. I am willing to admit that I have had it easier than some and that connection put me in a place of privilege, but it was never something I wanted. I want to earn my way, to build my own life just like my dad did. Like you have. Instead, I had to adapt to very different circumstances and have been trying to carefully distance myself ever since. I should have told you, though. At least about my record."

"I appreciate that, and I understand wanting to distance yourself from the expectations that come with that name. I was upset when I read about your record, but I am willing to admit that I overreacted and should have given you more of a chance to say your piece. I apologize for that. Can you forgive me?"

"Of course. Can you forgive me for not being honest with you upfront?"

"Of course."

Grace spotted her tablet resting on the console in front of her, so she grabbed it and started updating her self-imposed deadlines for her classes. Something nagged at the back of Dean's mind.

"There's more that's bothering you, isn't there?" he asked.

"It's nothing important."

"You can talk to me, Lieutenant."

"Please, call me Grace."

"Okay, Grace. What is it you aren't saying?"

"You mentioned that you're closest to Lucas Aemaris?"

"In the sense that he doesn't treat me like an outsider, yes. I wouldn't call us best friends, but we get along. Why?"

Grace sighed. "I served on a ship with him a while back. We were friendly, but he was much more interested in a friend of mine. She didn't feel the same and she confided in me in private that he is not her type. He didn't give up, though, even when she made it clear she wasn't interested. She and I were close, and we had been working our way towards a co-team lead position when he had her transferred out. I got promoted. She didn't. Everyone she worked with froze her out and she eventually ended up leaving the Fleet, just before we left. I think the only reason he started with her was because I was unavailable at the time."

"Oh Grace, I am so sorry. I know Lucas can be a bit of an ass sometimes, but I had no idea..."

"I'm pretty sure he's also why my girlfriend broke up with me, though I'm not sure how he orchestrated it."

"Convinced her you cheated on her with him, most likely..." Dean muttered. "Growing up in the environment he did, you get a certain air of entitlement that leads to a vindictive streak when you don't get what you want. Not that I am trying to excuse his behavior in the slightest. What he did was deplorable. You did nothing wrong, though."

"Oh, I know I didn't. That only makes it more unfair."

"Agreed."

"You're used to having to make excuses for them," Grace commented.

"Yeah, it's a bad habit I picked up when I spent more time in their company. I had to protect them if I wanted to be one of them. Thing is, I don't anymore but I still haven't fully kicked the habit."

"That's understandable. I'm sorry again for judging you so harshly. That was unfair. And I'm sorry for calling you a coward."

"You weren't entirely wrong, though. I've never been good at standing up for myself or speaking out against the things I've seen. It was a good reminder that I need to practice being a little braver."

"You're a good guy, Dean."

"Thanks, Grace. I try. I'll feel better once I figure out what's going on with the *Prism*. Are you good to stay here for a bit?"

"Yes. I've got my tablet, so I can work on some of my classes. Stay in touch via radio?"

"Of course. I shouldn't be long, but if you need me, I'll be here."

"I'll be fine, Dean. Just be safe."

"I will, Grace. I promise."

Personal Log, Dean Lindsay

I have a feeling I know why I was "removed" from the Fleet, but why would someone try and hurt Grace? It could be a simple case of someone trying to take out the competition, but the method feels extreme. They could have killed her.

I'm going to have to read carefully while I dig. Part of me wants to turn the beacon off, but I don't really have a good reason beyond bad vibes.

I wish my dad were here. He would know what to do.

Day 19

Personal Log, Grace Dillard

I am starting to have suspicions that I know are ridiculous, but they won't go away. Maybe it's the side effect of the CO2 poisoning. Either way, there is a voice in my head saying that Lucas has something to do with what is going on. I don't think he meant for things to escalate the way that they did, but maybe he arranged for Dean and I to be on lower-quality ships. Or maybe he put me somewhere isolated so he can be my knight in shining armor.

Either way, something feels strange. Something feels wrong. And I am going to find out what.

"That makes no sense. Are you sure you're reading that right?" Grace said. Whiskers II, the holo-cat, looked up from where they had been snoozing, startled by the sudden outburst.

"It's all right there." Dean handed her the tablet. "The *Prism* was overdue for repairs and upgrades to the life support system. The orders must have gotten lost in the shuffle."

"Is this something you can fix?"

"I can probably jury rig a replacement but at this point, it may not be enough to restore it to full functionality. Another idea is once that's been repaired and it's functioning properly, I can move the *Borealis* closer and we can connect the airlocks. That will take the pressure off and allow me to keep a closer eye on it."

"Can you do that?"

"It's been long enough since the last move, I'm confident I have enough stores to line up the airlocks. I won't be able to move it again for a while, but I don't think that'll be a problem."

"Okay. Let's do it then. How do I help?"

"I can handle this on my own."

"Of course you can, but I'm bored and want to help. So, how do I help?"

A smile spread across Dean's face, and he started to lay out his plan. Minutes later they were gathering their tools and suiting up. As they fell back into their old rhythm, Dean felt his spirits lifting as the weight vanished from his chest. The storms had finally stopped, and the sensors picked up no signs of their return, but they still moved with caution.

It took longer than it should have to fix the life support system this time. The damage didn't quite fit what Dean had expected, and he and Grace had to engage in some particularly clever problem-solving, but they eventually managed to get it working.

"Alright. Let's get the ships lined up and connected, then see how the fix is doing. I want to make sure it'll work before I hook everything up. Make sure there are no other surprises." Dean scrolled through the different diagnostic screens on his tablet and the console, glancing back and forth as if he were looking for something and not quite finding it.

"I don't think I'm quite so unlucky as to have multiple things wrong with my ship. Plus, you already checked things," Grace protested gently.

"I did, but it always pays to take extra precautions, especially in cases like this. Lots of unknown variables to account for."

"That makes sense. Better safe than sorry."

"Better safe than sorry."

Once Dean finished his checks, they began the slow, delicate dance of bringing the ships together. Then came more checks to ensure the connection was stable and the systems could handle the changes. By the end of the day, Dean declared that the airlocks were safe to open.

"Does this make us roommates?" Grace asked as he strolled from one ship to the other.

"I guess it does. We can do our agreements and boundaries tomorrow."

"Sounds good. Movie night?"

"Yes."

They returned to the designated movie room and settled into their usual seats, Dean handing Grace his tablet to allow her to select the movie. Whiskers II followed a few paces behind her and curled up at her feet, falling 'asleep' once more. She looked at the next movie on her mental watchlist, an espionage thriller, but something in the description hit a little too close to home so she chose something more lighthearted instead. She needed something comforting, something familiar, something that would help soothe the unease that bubbled in the pit of her stomach.

Dean didn't protest or question her choice in the slightest, though that was more because he was far too stuck in his own thoughts, trying to piece things together.

"Earth to Dean," she said gently, "come in, Dean."

"Huh, what?"

"You looked a little lost there. Is everything alright?"

"Yeah, sorry. Just got a lot on my mind, trying to figure out what's going on and what we need to do and…" he trailed off as she reached over and placed her hand on top of his.

"I know, I've been thinking about it too, but we both need a break if we are going to make it through this. You're no good to me burnt out, and vice versa. Let's just relax, enjoy a good show, then get some rest. The problem will still be there in the morning, and we can get back to it once we are refreshed."

"When did you become so knowledgeable about mental health? I thought that was my thing?" he protested playfully.

"When I ran out of other classes and decided to borrow some of yours. Plus, it seemed like a good topic to brush up on, given our current situation. The kinds of stressors we are facing can really do a number on the brain."

"That they can. Good thing we are two of the smartest people in the Fleet. Or, at least one of us is. I'm just stubborn."

She pulled back her hand and swatted his arm playfully, and he reacted with great dramatic flair as if he had been punched. This sent both of them into a fit of giggles that lasted long enough that the movie began to play by itself.

They soon found themselves lost in a fantastic world that they had known since they were very young. The familiarity brought comfort and a small sense of nostalgia, but not enough to bring the pain. No, it brought them a sense of peace and rest.

Grace fell asleep during the credits, and Dean joined her during the director's commentary.

Personal Log, Dean Lindsay

I used to think that when this was all done and we were off this planet, Grace and I would go our separate ways. Now, knowing what I know about how we ended up here, I don't want to let her out of my sight. I worry about her, even though I know she is strong enough to handle anything. I don't want to see her hurt. I want to see her happy. I want to see her safe.

I want to keep being her friend after this, to keep her as part of my life. She's pretty amazing.

Maybe once we get off this planet and are connected to civilization again, I will ask her to have dinner somewhere nice. Just see how things go. At the very least it can be how I say thanks for keeping me sane through all of this.

Day 22

Dear Mom,

You know how you were always encouraging me to get an apartment with a roommate and I swore I would never? Well, turns out you were right about that, just like you were about so many other things.

Dean hasn't moved onto my ship so much as we found a way to connect our ships. It's like having a really big apartment, but without having to pay rent. Sure, the space is bigger, but it doesn't feel as empty. Also, Dean is a surprisingly good roommate. I wasn't sure about him at first, but he is definitely starting to grow on me. You are going to have to meet him when we get home.

~~If we ever get home.~~ I am choosing to stay positive. We will figure this out. We won't be trapped here forever.

I will see you again, and when I do, I will introduce you to Dean and to Whiskers the Second. He's an absolute sweety, and he doesn't shed.

I am talking about the cat, not Dean. Though Dean is very sweet. Not sure about the shedding.

Having the two ships connected ended up having a much larger impact on their quality of life than either of them expected.

Dean no longer had to put on and take off the suit multiple times in one day and Grace got the chance to spend more time on the *Borealis*, which was great when she needed a change of scenery. It also helped even the workload for both ship systems, allowing Dean to route some of the power cache to auxiliary storage.

They settled into a new rhythm, existing in their shared space with a level of comfort that surprised Grace. Boundaries were quickly established, and duties were divided without much of a fuss. Sure, they had their differences, but they also had a lot in common and at the end of the day, they really did trust each other.

"I passed!" Dean exclaimed one day. They were in the media room, curled up on their respective couches, working through some classes.

"You did?"

"Yep! I am officially halfway through the engineering certification program."

"That's amazing, Dean! You've been working on that what, a week?"

"More like two."

"Impressive...wait, how long have we been here?"

"I believe today would be day twenty-one. Twenty-two?"

"Twenty-two days and no word back from the Fleet," Grace's voice cracked. "Didn't you say they would send a response after the second week?"

"I said they would most likely send something when they reached the asteroid belt. It was my best guess based on the information I had, but things could have changed since our crash. Any number of things could have slowed them down."

"The days here are longer than those measured by the Fleet. We should have heard something by now. Tell me the truth, Dean. No one's coming, are they."

"I don't think they are, Grace," Dean admitted softly. "We would have heard something by now. I've been watching the internal communications as they update and there's been no mention of what happened. I don't know for sure, but it doesn't look like they heard our beacon. It's going to be okay, though. We have supplies. We have plenty of energy. We crashed on a mostly hospitable planet. We can either keep waiting or we can find our own way off this planet."

"As nice as this planet is, I'd rather not spend the rest of my life here. I haven't given up on my dreams yet."

"Those dreams may not work out exactly like you want it to, but I get the feeling that's not going to stop you."

"Nope. It's like my mom always says, never stop dreaming until you reach the stars."

"Let's get to it, then. We have a lot of work to do if we are going to get these ships space-worthy."

And so, they got to work. First, they had to do an inventory of everything they had, from food to water to physical supplies. Then they had to do a thorough check of both ships inside and out. Assessing their readiness would take a lot of work and no small amount of research, as well as some extra materials. They started with the basics and pieced together a plan for the rest.

It would take as long as it needed to take, and they would keep going until they got to the stars.

As they worked, they talked. They talked about the places they had been, the dreams they had chased, their fondest memories. They also talked about what they wanted to do when they finished their tour with the Fleet.

"There are plenty of places you can go after the Survey Corps. Why the Settlement Board?" Dean asked.

"For one, being a member of the Settlement Board comes with a lot of useful perks and financial security. I'll be able to move my mom somewhere really nice where she doesn't have to work if she doesn't want to. There might also be part of me that wants to do it because it's supposed to be hard to get into."

"You do seem to have a bit of a competitive streak, but not one of the ones where you push other people down on your way up. I respect that."

"And what about you? What's your interest in engineering?"

"I've always enjoyed fixing and making things. Then after what happened with my parents, I wanted to see if I could make things safer. Build things better and make things easier to fix. I wondered for a long time if maybe they would have made it had the shuttle been in better shape. That's part of why I now know so much about ship repair, but it's also something I really do enjoy."

"You are pretty good at it, too."

"Thanks!"

They settled into a comfortable silence for a few minutes as they focused on compiling a list of the materials they would need to gather and the projects that would need to be completed before testing the flight worthiness of the ships.

"You know," Grace said after a while, "I have also thought about being a teacher or perhaps a researcher."

"Oh really?" Dean prodded.

"Yeah, it's not quite as glamorous and doesn't pay as well, but I do enjoy it. There are so many wonderful things out there that we haven't even begun to understand. Studying the samples we have collected here has been absolutely fascinating even though I can only make sense of about half of what I find. I still have a long way to go before I can be considered a botanist."

"You can do anything you set your mind to, Grace, and knowing you, whatever you end up doing you are going to be amazing at it. And your mom is going to be so very proud of you."

"Thanks, Dean. It helps to hear that."

"Any time, Grace. Now, tell me, if you could take a vacation anywhere in the home system, where would it be?"

"There's this little planet I remember a friend telling me about. You can't walk on the surface due to the consistency and the heat, but the atmosphere is clear enough that you can fly over and see the entire history of it etched into the swirling surface. One of the names for it is God's Marble."

"Doesn't sound exactly like a vacation spot."

"Well, the planet isn't but there are a few stations nearby that are..."

They kept working until the sun started to go down, then they returned to the ships that had become their home. Grace went to sleep quickly, but Dean stayed up to gather his thoughts on what needed to be done next.

Personal Log, Dean Lindsay

The timing might be tight, but I am pretty confident that we can pull this off. I think if we can reposition portions of the hull of the Borealis, *then we can lessen the strain on the life support systems and decrease the possibility of a breach. I know it may sound like I'm being emotional, but with everything that's been going on, I feel better having both ships with us when we leave. We can drop the* Borealis *if we need to and we will be just fine, I'm just...paranoid.*

And maybe a little nostalgic. This is the first thing that's felt like it's mine. I don't want to lose it. But I'd also much rather get back to the home system and find something that feels a bit more like home.

Day 25

Hey mom!

25 days into being stranded on this strange, but very pretty planet, and we finally have a plan for how we are going to leave. We have some final checks we need to run before we are ready to start working, of course. Must take precautions when preparing for space travel. While this detour was not part of my plan, it has been very educational. Turns out I make a pretty good mechanic. Which is good, because that means we can get more work done faster when it's time to start on repairs.

I am one step closer to coming home. Hope to see you soon.

Grace

Once they had all of the information they needed, they came up with a plan. According to Dean's estimates, it would take at least a week to get the *Prism* back in flying condition. Fixing the *Borealis* would take months, assuming there were enough materials available to repair the portions of the hull that were dented by the trees.

"I am going to run some structural integrity tests on the hulls, if you wouldn't mind pulling up past repair reports while I do that," Dean said.

"Are you sure you don't want me out there with you?" Grace asked.

"I can run the first round using the external sensors. If nothing pops up there, then tomorrow I will do a second round using some of your survey equipment. I'll just need to make a few adjustments."

"Understood. I will get started on repair reports. You let me know if there's anything else I can help with."

"Will do."

Even with both of their tinkering with the systems, the intranet took minutes to load what normally would have taken seconds. To save herself some time, Grace clicked to access three months' worth of reports at once, then busied herself with her book while the computer chugged away.

"I've got the files, Dean," Grace called an hour later. "Past three months. Am I looking for anything in particular?"

"Looking for any repair requests that were made in that time period and what was done, as well as any routine maintenance that was performed and when. It'll help prioritize what needs to be fixed."

"On it." She started scrolling through the reports, brow furrowing more and more as she read. "Hey, Dean?"

The concern rang so clearly in her voice that he almost quite literally dropped what he was doing. He slowed long enough to set his tools down somewhere secure before running across the ships to find Grace exactly where he had left her.

"What's wrong?" he demanded.

"Look at this."

He pulled a chair over to sit next to her, scrutinizing the documents she had open with an equally furrowed brow. She slid over to give him more room to navigate as he scrolled through the very same documents that had caught her attention. Then he scrolled back through the logs, face growing more and more stoic.

"Where did you get these?" he asked finally.

"Since I am technically the captain of this vessel, I can access the back-end engineering and tech reports for the *Prism* and when you gave me your credentials, I was able to do the same for the *Borealis*."

"And what did your front-end reports show?"

"That everything was fine and had been properly updated at the last inspection."

"Same here, which means either the people who make the reports are missing important information, or they are intentionally leaving those details out. Both of those options are bad."

"Why would anyone leave details like that out of a report? Issues pertaining to life support are to be dealt with immediately and reported to the Fleet."

"It could be something as simple as a miscommunication or there could have been money, or favors involved. I can't say for sure until I've had a chance to dig deeper. Can you keep looking through these and flag everything that was not included in the reports you received? I need to finish the integrity tests, then I want to dig into the history of the *Borealis*."

"Do you think this could be the cause of the crash?"

"Possibly. Can't know for sure until I have the full picture," Dean muttered, eyes locked on the screen.

The next few hours he and Grace focused on the reports, chasing down the threads, forgetting about the quest to repair the ships. They had answers to find, buried as they were in strange places, hidden behind confusing folder names. Almost like someone went out of their way to make sure the truth would be hard to find.

"It looks like the last two times the *Prism* underwent inspection, the valve was flagged as needing replacement. Both requests were denied, and when the tech tried to push the subject, they were transferred to another ship and it looks like the part order was erased from the system," Grace said. "This is unbelievable."

"I hate to say it, but that sounds like a lot more than just negligence. The question is why?"

"Did you spot anything strange with the *Borealis*?"

"Everything looks perfectly fine, including things I know I had to repair myself over the past few months. It's almost like someone submitted the exact same report with a few alterations every month."

"Why would someone do that?"

"To hide something would be my guess. I for one am much more interested in knowing who did it and what they are hiding. I am probably going to have to break a few rules to find any answers. I completely understand if you'd prefer some plausible deniability."

"I think if there's someone out there trying to sabotage other members of the Fleet, we need to find out who sooner rather than later. Exceptions have been made for rules that were bent to help protect the Fleet," Grace commented.

"Oh, I am well aware of some of the loopholes that exist within the Fleet. I've also picked up a few tricks in my tinkering that I can use to keep this discreet. I just don't want to mess up your chances for promotion more than I already have."

"What do you mean by that?"

Dean sighed. "I might have had a falling out with Lucas that didn't get resolved before the Fleet left, and I was never in great standing with the rest of the family. There's no telling what someone might have decided to do in response. That family has politics like you wouldn't believe."

"You're telling me that your accident might not have been an accident? You think someone intentionally sabotaged your ship to make it crash?"

"I can't speak to their specific end goal, but I am pretty damn sure that at least part of my engine failure was intentional…"

"What are you not saying, Dean?" Grace demanded. His face twisted into an unpleasant expression as he pulled out his tablet and opened his messenger. Everyone in the Fleet had one but neither of theirs had been working properly since the crash.

"This is the message Lucas sent me a few minutes before things went boom. They only loaded properly about an hour ago."

There were two messages sent within seconds of each other, moments before Dean crashed into Grace.

Duck.

You should have left it alone.

Ice flooded her veins. His words echoed in her mind, mingling with all of the rumors that floated around the Aemaris family and families like them. The lengths to which people in power will go to maintain that power, and to remove anything and anyone that might be a threat. Her breaths came shallow and fast as her mind raced and raced and raced and she descended further and further into panic. Dean moved towards her, concern written all over his face.

"He...they...that's why no one's coming. You're not supposed to come back. I'm not supposed to come back. They tried to kill you and now they are going to leave you here to die and I'm just stuck being collateral damage and now my mom is going to be all alone and who knows what they are going to tell her happened to me and-"

"Grace, breathe. I know this is a scary situation, but we are in this together and we will figure this out. Just look at me and breathe with me, please. In through the nose and out through the mouth, deep and slow. Okay?"

"Okay," she choked out between gasps.

Dean started breathing, exaggerating the movements as she tried to copy him. It took a few minutes but gradually she regained control of her breathing, though her hands continued to shake.

"I have some very mild sedatives if you would like something to take the edge off and help you get your panic under control. That is entirely your choice. Whatever you think will help."

"I think I just need some quiet to process things. If you need me, I'll be in my room."

"Okay. I will give you space but if you need anything, don't hesitate to ask. Even if it's just someone to be in the same space. Whatever you need."

"Alone. Alone sounds good." Grace stood slowly and walked off in the direction of her quarters.

Dean didn't move, but he watched to make sure she got there safely, not looking away until the door had been closed for a few seconds. With no one else to see, he didn't bother trying to hide his worry. The situation was worse than he thought and now, because of him, Grace could be in danger. The idea had never occurred to him but now it burrowed in his brain and the guilt would not let go. He needed to find out what was going on.

He needed to fix this before things got even more out of control. So, he kept digging, carefully breaking every rule in the Fleet to try and find what he needed. To try and find answers.

Grace didn't feel much like talking even after she managed to pull herself together. Dean ended up bribing her out of her quarters with promises of candy and movies, just to make sure she ate something. As with the last movie night, she fell asleep on the couch soon after the movie ended. Then she woke under a jacket and went up to the helm to curl up in the chair across from Dean.

Dean had not been asleep, but he pretended to be until her breathing deepened and evened as she drifted off to sleep. On this night he was far too restless to sleep so easily. He needed to do something, to accomplish something simple, to add a little hope in the light of all they had learned.

After several minutes of staring pointlessly at the ceiling, he remembered Grace talking about some special night-blooming plants she had been wanting to study. The sun had only just dipped below the horizon, so he reasoned that it would be safe for a quick trip out and about to gather some samples for her.

He quickly slipped into one of the surveyor suits and grabbed one of the sample kits that Grace always carried with her on their walks, pausing only long enough to leave her a note. He didn't want to frighten her, just surprise her.

Stepping out into the night felt like stepping into a different world entirely. A vast array of stars stretched overhead, a dizzying blanket of lights twinkling in the sky, providing a smattering of light to complement the gray landscape. Dean took care to keep the ships in sight as he wound his way through the brush and trees, taking samples here and there of the flowers that only bloomed during the night.

He had crouched down to dig up some roots that Grace liked when he realized he was not alone. Something was watching him. Something large, and from the sound of the growl slipping from the shadows, it was not happy to see him.

Dean tried to play it off like he hadn't noticed and began packing his things back into his pockets, mentally calculating the best way to get back to the ships without incurring the wrath of whatever he had awakened.

The creature followed him, though, and right as he stepped into the clearing, it attacked.

It slammed Dean to the ground with enough force to drive the air from his lungs, claws digging deep into his back, nearly puncturing his suit. He rolled over, trying to get his feet between the creature and himself to throw it off.

He got a vicious bite to the arm for his troubles and more claws to the ribs. He screamed in pain, trying to wriggle out from underneath the beast. It shied back from the sound, and he cried out again, this time in anger.

The creature wrenched Dean's arm one last time before running off, taking a chunk of his suit with it.

"Okay. That was a bad idea," Dean muttered to himself. "Certainly not my finest moment. Owww that hurt. That hurt a lot. My arm is definitely broken. Oh wow, Grace is not going to let me live this down. That was a spectacularly bad idea. Okay, let's get back inside and get to the med bay."

He slowly hauled himself to his feet and staggered over to the *Borealis* airlock, where he punched in the key code to open the door.

The light flashed red.

He tried it again.

The light flashed red.

He tried an older code.

Same response.

He swore, then tried his commander's override code.

The light flashed red.

"Okay, that's really bad," Dean said, leaning back against the ship and running through all of the possible reasons that his codes wouldn't work. The only conclusion he could come to was that either there was a weird glitch going on or someone had enacted a high-level lockdown of the entire Fleet.

He tried another code, one of Grace's, and got the same response. That confirmed it. The Fleet was on lockdown, and he had no way of getting into either ship until Grace let him back in. It also meant they would have a lot of work to do to keep control from disappearing completely.

Dean slid to the ground with his back against the airlock door and recorded a message for himself as a reminder of what would need to be done when he woke up. Then he tried to hail Grace.

No response.

Until they got control back, there would be no communication. He just had to wait and trust that Grace would know what to do when she found him.

Day 26

The next morning, Grace woke up alone.

"Dean?" she called, confused. The sun had not yet risen, though the clock told her it would in a few hours. The ships were quiet. Too quiet. "Dean?"

She sat up, reaching for the light controls on the wall. The chair still had an indentation from where Dean slept, but he wasn't there. Instead, her tablet rested on the seat. This caught her attention because that was most certainly not where she left it.

She tapped the screen to turn it on. It lit up immediately, and a recently received message appeared on the screen.

I stepped outside briefly to collect some of those night-blooming plants you were wanting to study. I have my communicator with me, and I will be back soon. I hope you slept well. Everything is going to be okay. - Dean

The weight vanished off her shoulders to be replaced by a warmth in her chest. She would give anything to not be stuck in this situation, but at least she had Dean with her. Something about having him by her side made things feel a little less impossible.

She sent a reply expressing her thanks and offering to fix breakfast, then settled back into her seat to watch the sunrise. The coziness caused her to doze off briefly, but her morning alarm woke her before she could miss the show. Dean had still not returned.

The colors began to paint the sky in the same dazzling display as many mornings before, though Grace still had not grown tired of the spectacle. As the light drifted down from the sky to the ground, however, she began to realize something was different this morning.

She sat up straighter to get a better look at the churned-up dirt and ripped up plants in front of the ship. At first, she thought the disturbance came from a hog-like creature rooting around for vegetation.

Then she saw the streak of blood, and the torn pieces of suit dotting the grass.

"Dean!" She leapt to her feet and made a mad dash for the airlock, grabbing a breather along the way. Suiting up would waste time she didn't have but she would be no good to anyone unconscious.

The doors took forever to open, but when they finally did, she stopped short of leaping through them. Dean groaned as he slumped back into the airlock chamber, bleeding and not fully conscious.

"Oh, my stars, Dean!" Grace exclaimed.

"Grace?" he rasped, trying to look at her.

"I'm here, Dean. It's okay. You're okay. Is anything broken? Can you move?"

"Leg...sprain..."

"Okay. I am going to grab you under your arms and pull you back into the airlock, okay? Then we can start patching you up enough to get you to the med bay."

He mumbled something that she took as an agreement and started carefully hauling him back onto the ship, glad that he had decided to pass out near the *Borealis* door and not the *Prism*. That would have been a much longer journey back to the med bay.

Grace surveyed his injuries while the airlock sealed and adjusted the pressurization, trying to figure out what needed to be treated first. He was covered in scratches with a couple of bite marks on his legs. The arm he had curled across his chest had a bend where there shouldn't have been.

"Okay, Dean. I am going to run to the med bay to get some supplies. You just keep breathing for me, okay?" she said, gently shifting him into what she hoped was a more comfortable position.

"Gurney...cabinet..." he muttered.

"There's a gurney in the cabinet? Is it one of the ones that hovers?" she asked. He nodded. "Perfect. I will be right back, I promise."

She scampered out of the airlock, nearly tripping over her own feet in her mad dash to get to the med bay. It took a few minutes to find and activate the gurney. By then she was in such a rush she grabbed a couple of emergency med kits and booked it to get back to Dean.

He was still breathing when she got back, drifting in and out of consciousness.

"Alright, first things first, stop the bleeding then look for infection. I also need to stabilize that arm until we can get you back to the med bay. This is going to be unpleasant, but I will be as gentle as I can, I promise," she said.

Her first challenge was to get Dean out of the remains of the suit. She ended up having to cut the sleeve off to avoid causing any more damage to his already broken arm. That proved tricky and only mostly successful. The rest was easier.

"I am so glad you sent me those emergency medical courses, otherwise I would be a lot more panicked right now," Grace muttered. "I mean, I am still panicking but it's a much more controlled panic because I have some idea what I am doing. Granted, most of my knowledge is theoretical but I've always been good at applying theoretical knowledge in practical situations. My instructors always said I work well under pressure. Well, all except for one but he was just an ass. If only he could see me now."

She kept up a pleasant conversation, shifting from topic to topic, trying to keep it interesting to keep him awake. He perked up some after she hooked him up to some fluids and a blood transfusion, with the help of the automated assistant.

"You're doing great, Grace." His words came softly and less garbled with pain.

"I am glad you think so. I've always been a fan of having practical experience, but I was hoping for a less trial by fire approach. What happened?" she asked, carefully sliding his broken arm into a half cast to keep it steady while she worked on it.

"First thing, this is Acting Captain Dean Lindsay naming Lieutenant Grace Dillard as Acting Chief Medic of the *Borealis* under emergency circumstances. Code is Foxtrot Alpha Charlie One Niner Niner," he said clearly. Several lights flashed briefly in confirmation. "There, now the things will listen to you. The assistant can get you anything you need, like an x-ray."

"Wonderful. Kir, I would like to get an x-ray of Dean's arm please. We need to make sure it's properly set and there's no complications before I put a cast on." A panel detached from the ceiling and lowered until it was a foot above Dean's arm. "Excellent. Thank you. Now, Dean, tell me what happened."

Dean talked while she worked, the words tumbling out one after another as he fought to keep his eyes open. "I was having trouble sleeping, so I decided I needed to do something to get the energy out. There wasn't much I could do on the ship without waking you, so I decided to go on a quick trip outside. You had mentioned before wanting to get a sample of the night-blooming plants that we saw during the storm, so I went to go and collect some for you to study. Saw some other interesting things out there so after I brought some back, I went to investigate. Ended up having an unexpected and rather unpleasant encounter with what must have been a very territorial, nocturnal creature. You could say it took a lot out of me. Couldn't quite manage to let myself in so I figured I'd hang out by the door until you came to get me."

Some of his words slipped out through clenched teeth as she carefully adjusted his arm to line up the fractured bones.

"Well, the good news is the break looks clean and I'm not seeing any additional damage. If you want to double check in case, I missed something, I will get the rest of the cast and some pain medicine." She tilted the x-ray so Dean could see it, then went back to the cabinet.

"Looks good. Maybe check again later, though. My vision's kind of fuzzy...or is it my focus?"

"Hopefully it's just the second one. Now, hold still while I clean up and bandage your arm before I put the rest of the cast on. This isn't going to feel good, but it'll feel better than an infection."

"Can you tell me a story-" he hissed as the first drop of antiseptic hit his skin. "Something to keep my mind off things."

"Sure, I have lots of stories from the different field studies I did when I was still a junior member in the Survey Corps," Grace said, taking great care to wipe the blood off his injured arm so she could see where the wounds were. "Most of the assignments looked incredibly boring on paper but there were some really interesting things that never made it into the reports. Like one time, we were out collecting soil samples, and we came across signs of some sort of burrowing creature. Naturally, we had to investigate, to ensure the area was safe and because we were bored of collecting soil samples. Someone got the brilliant idea to strap a camera onto a root analyzer and feed it through the holes to see if we could find the creature..."

Dean clung to Grace's stories, using her words in his battle to stay conscious even when his body begged for rest or oblivion. Once his arm was set and fully engulfed in the cast the pain became significantly more tolerable. Even so, she kept talking, kept him from drifting to sleep, kept cleaning and treating the rest of his wounds.

"And there we go," she said. "That should hold you for now. Your vitals look good. Why don't you get some rest, and I'll check on your bandages in a few hours?"

Dean was already fast asleep by the time she finished her question. Content that she had done everything she could for the time being,

Grace dimmed the lights and settled into the nearby chair. She read one of her adventures while Dean slept, eventually drifting off to sleep herself, until KIR woke her to check on Dean.

Day 27

Grace spent most of the 27th day pouring through every medical resource she could find, trying to find a way to combat the various infections Dean had in the scratches and bites. When she did a closer inspection of his suit, she found small tears in the fabric that didn't go all the way through, but when she swabbed both sides, she knew some sort of bacteria or fungal something got through where the bite mark was. Whatever it was, it was aggressive and had plenty of time to settle into Dean's system.

His fever spiked during the night and while she couldn't get rid of it completely, she at least managed to lower it to a less dangerous temperature. She left KIR watching him on the highest alert while she frantically tried to run tests on what substances she could find in the wounds and on the bandages.

He didn't give her much time, though. First, she had to get him stable. Then she could save his life.

There was also the matter of the message Dean had recorded, warning of the lockdown. Whenever she wasn't frantically playing nurse, she followed his instructions to ensure that she would not lose control of her ship. He tried to help, pushing past his mental haze to walk her through some of the more complicated parts.

It took most of the day, but she managed to put a program in place that would allow her to override any lockdown protocols for at least a few days. It would have to do until she could get Dean back on his feet enough for him to take a crack at it.

Day 28

Grace moved the bulk of her scientific equipment into the med bay during the brief periods that Dean slept peacefully. The antibiotics were starting to help on the scratches, but the bites remained stubbornly infected.

"Why is nothing working?" she exclaimed after, yet another treatment failed to make a difference. The virtual assistant didn't have the advancements necessary to deal with such a complex problem, leaving it to Grace to find a way to fix it.

So, she turned to the one thing she knew she could count on. Science.

"If the bite infection is different, that either means different bacteria or some kind of venom, which means I just need to figure out what gets rid of it. I can do that."

After making sure Dean would be okay for the next few hours, Grace gathered some things, including both her survey pack and Dean's emergency medical pack. She also made sure to tuck a stunner into her belt, just in case.

Feeling adequately prepared, she did one last test of the override protocol to make sure she'd be able to get back onto the ship. Then she grabbed the physical unlock control for the *Prism*, just in case.

"I'll be back, Dean," she said. "Just hang in there for me." He didn't respond. Not that she expected him to.

She exited the *Borealis* through the door where she had found Dean and began to follow the faint trail left behind by the creature that had attacked him. Time had worn much of it away, but there were still traces of blood from where the creature itself had become injured. Between that and the fact she had been tracking some of its nightly movements via the survey drones, she was able to find its den without too much issue.

Grace crept carefully inside, pulling some swabs from her survey kit. The creature slept peacefully, unaware of any intrusion as she leaned over it and gently put the swabs in its mouth one at a time, getting samples from its teeth and gums. She took some samples from under its claws as well. The creature itself reminded her of a bobcat, except much more muscular and with scales instead of fur. Though when she took the samples from the mouth, she noticed signs of what could be a frill around its neck. An interesting trait for her to consider the purpose of once she had Dean back on the mend.

Being away from him for this long made her nervous. She had played the part of nurse to the best of her ability, but she was far from a medical expert. As she entered the *Prism*, samples in hand, she clung to the hope that she would find the answer she needed.

Dean remained asleep, likely unaware of her absence. She checked his vitals, which were holding steady even if they were far from what she considered to be ideal. At least his condition hadn't worsened in the few minutes he was alone.

"Okay, let's see what we have to work with," she muttered to herself as she settled back into her makeshift lab. "This should at the very least make it easier for me to narrow down what sort of treatments will work without having to worry about cross-reactions making things worse. Some of these things you have to be very careful when combining, but I am confident that between myself and KIR we will find a treatment that works."

She continued talking as she worked, explaining her process to Dean and regaling him with stories she had learned in her survey training. Sometimes she paused to narrate her research as she checked that her work would not kill him.

He remained mostly oblivious, but it brought Grace some comfort to think it all out loud.

She did not sleep that night.

Day 29

Grace implemented her treatment plan after pulling an all-nighter with KIR as her only real company. After her self-mandated lunch break, Grace changed Dean's bandages. Then she sat down and promptly fell asleep.

Day 30

Grace woke with a start at the sound of her name, bolting upright in the bed to find Dean blinking blearily at her.

"You're awake!" she exclaimed, rushing over. "And you're looking so much better. How do you feel?"

"I know I've felt better, but it's been a while since that was true. What happened?"

"You were attacked by a nocturnal animal. You were badly injured when I found you and your wounds got infected. I had to go and get a sample from the creature's mouth, but I was able to get enough to find a treatment. It's been added to the record."

"How long was I out?"

"I found you on the morning of the 26th day, and it's about midday on the 30th."

"Oh. That's a long time...wait, did you say you got a sample from its mouth?"

"Yep. It left quite the trail back to its den. The tricky part was getting close to its mouth without waking its cubs. Nothing I couldn't handle, though."

"You really are something, Grace. Seriously, I don't know how many people would have had the guts to do something like that, or the smarts."

"It was nothing. I only did what I had to do. You would have done the same if it was me."

"I'm a good medic but it would never occurred to me to follow the trail back to its den-"

"Dean, don't you dare downplay your intelligence. You are smart. You would have figured it out."

"Regardless, I don't have to because you did. You solved it. You saved my life."

"Does this make us even? You saved my life, now I saved yours."

"First off, I would have died in the *Borealis* in a matter of days if you hadn't been there to let me out, so I'd argue that I still owe you one. Second, I'd never hold that over you. No strings or expectations. Third, if this makes us anything, I hope it makes us friends."

"Absolutely." She flashed him a brilliant smile and gently took his hand in hers. "No question. Well, one question. Do you want to try eating something?"

"Sure," he chuckled. "I can give it a shot. I could use some water too."

"Excellent. I will be right back."

She gave his hand a squeeze before scurrying out of the room. He took advantage of the silence to try and come to terms with the fact he had very nearly died. The part that upset him the most was the fact that he would have left Grace alone on this strange planet. He couldn't do that to her. He also couldn't lose her.

She came back with his tablet tucked under one arm, holding a handful of rations and candy, along with two canteens. A smile spread across his face, sparking a similar smile to appear on hers as she set her things down on the nearest table.

"I was thinking we could have a movie night in here, since you're feeling better. I figured out how to move the cots around and how to use the wall projector," she said excitedly.

"There's a wall projector?"

"You didn't know? Most places like this have them. They're usually used for displaying diagnostics for study, but with some tweaking you can project other things. I might have played some cooking shows while you slept. I needed some background noise."

"I had no idea. They usually stuck me on triage or the emergency wing. I never got the chance to learn much of the long-term health tech, outside of doing my own study. I should work on that."

"Well, good news is now you have a chance. Your arm is healing nicely, but it's still very broken and you're still very injured. You're going to be on bed rest for a while. Plenty of time to study."

"Mmmmm any chance I can get out early for good behavior?"

"The more you rest, the faster you heal, the sooner you can get back to your work," she said firmly.

"Fine, fine. You do outrank me."

"Yes, I do. And not only that, but I'm technically your doctor so you have even more reason to listen to me. Now here, find us something to watch while I get myself set up."

"Yes, ma'am." He gave her a crisp salute, which made her laugh for the first time in days. She handed him the tablet, and he opened it immediately, scrolling through his library with one hand, using the cast to prop it up.

By the time she had herself situated he had the movie ready to play.

"This one is a bit of a long one, and an odd one, but I promise it's worth it," he explained.

"Sounds good. While we watch, see if you can eat this protein bar. Fluids can only do so much."

"Yes, ma'am." He gave her a mock salute and nearly dropped his tablet in surprise when she responded with a rude gesture and a mischievous smile. Then he hit the button to start the movie.

They spent the rest of the day watching movies and shows, interspersed with Grace fussing over Dean. After the first movie she made him get up and walk to the restroom, which ended up being a good idea. if an awkward one.

By nightfall they were both so tired that neither was awake when the credits rolled.

Day 31

Grace woke to find Dean watching her. Not only that, but he was sitting up with a cup of rehydrated coffee in his hand.

"Good morning, sunshine," he said, handing her the mug.

"Good morning. What time is it?"

"It's about three hours past sunrise. I've been up for two of those. You were sleeping so soundly I couldn't bring myself to wake you. I have been taking care not to push myself too far, but I did do a little walking around. I figured you'd appreciate some coffee."

"Thank you." She pushed herself into a seated position, having a good stretch before reaching to accept the mug. "I didn't know we had much left."

"We don't, but I figured given recent events a bit of a splurge was worth it. At least with the luxury things like coffee. We still need to be careful with rations."

"I am inclined to agree." She took a slow, grateful sip. "I have been taking care to stick to our ration schedule, so we still have enough to last us another week or so at our current rate of consumption. We will need to figure out another solution soon. How are you feeling today?"

"I still feel a bit like a deflated balloon but moving doesn't hurt as much, so that's nice. Also, kind of thirsty."

"Let me get you some water. We have enough drinkable water to last for two, maybe three days. In the meantime, I took a field trip to the river to collect more. It's in the process of being purified. I've got plans if it doesn't work but we should be fine."

"On the ball as always," Dean commented.

"I had to do something to keep myself occupied while you slept. Plus, some things needed to be taken care of sooner rather than later. I even tried to do some maintenance things, though I wasn't able to do much about your to-do list."

"We can worry about that when I'm back on my feet. Plus, who knows, maybe we will get picked up soon and someone else can deal with it."

"I turned off the beacon," Grace admitted.

"You what?" Dean nearly choked on his coffee.

"I can always turn it back on, but I just thought with everything that's been going on we should take a minute to think through things."

"I feel like I know you pretty well by now, Grace, even though we've only known each other for a month. Something big must have happened to shake your trust in the Fleet. What happened? What did I miss? I can tell you've been dancing around something since I woke up."

"What do you know about Jump Point Tarsis?"

Dean's brow furrowed in confusion, then his eyes widened in surprise as Grace continued to look at him, waiting for a response.

"What about it?" he asked.

"I think it might be related to the crash. The last time I saw Lucas, I overheard him talking to someone, and he mentioned the word, Tarsis. I didn't think anything of it until he yelled at me for eavesdropping. Then, when you were feverish, you were mumbling things and one of the words I heard you repeat was Tarsis. So, I looked it up in the Fleet archives. The records say it's an old jump point that hasn't been used in decades, but I get the feeling it's something more. What do you know about it?"

"Well, you know how the rebellion broke off from the Empire during the ceasefire, fleeing to the outskirts of known space to start over somewhere outside of the Empire's reach? The group that broke off was so big that they had to split up into different Fleets and take different routes to get to where we ended up. They didn't want to risk the Empire being able to follow. Only one person per Fleet knew where to go, and once everyone arrived, they erased all knowledge of their paths and shut down every jump point but one, in case there were any stragglers.

"Jump Point Tarsis?" Grace asked.

"Could be. I learned most of this from being around the Aemaris family. I did a little digging of my own, but I never found anything definitive. I don't know who, if anyone, knew which gate was left intact. Assuming there even was one. You said you heard Lucas mention it?"

"Yes. I don't remember the exact context but the bit that stuck with me was something about a detour to Tarsis. I thought we were headed for the Myron asteroid field to play hide and seek with the Empire, but when I looked at old star charts Tarsis is nowhere near there."

"You don't think..." Dean's voice trailed off as his eyes grew distant.

"You have an idea, don't you?" Grace prodded.

"Yes, and it is going to require doing things for which we will have absolutely no plausible deniability if or when we get caught."

"Pretty sure your brother and his friends will find something to frame us for. Might as well get in trouble for something we did do."

"In that case, how would you like to learn how to hack?"

"I would love to." Grace tried to project a confidence that she didn't necessarily feel. To her, hacking had always seemed to be a dangerous, difficult thing. Something she would never do. Considering the circumstances, though, she was willing to bend that rule, so long as she didn't go invading anyone's privacy.

Hours later, they were metaphorically elbows deep in data, carefully combing through to find anything that could be helpful. The going was slow, but progress was steady as they wound their way through the different layers of security. Dean managed to disable parts of the Fleet's AI to prevent it from triggering a security lockdown, which could have proven incredibly problematic. Even so, they had to tread with care.

"You are surprisingly good at this," Dean commented after a long stretch of silence.

"Thanks. I've always been a fast learner."

"And you said you have no previous coding experience?"

"Unless you count my troubleshooting the survey equipment, which usually required a lot of fiddling to get it to work correctly in different environments," Grace said, not making eye contact.

"Are you sure? Because I never told you how to bypass that subroutine, and you did it flawlessly."

Grace froze in the middle of her typing for half a second before continuing, not wanting to lose her place. "I may have picked up a few things here or there in order to ensure my educational plans remained on track. Some classes have unnecessarily complicated requirements for entering and I didn't exactly have the same support system as the rest of my classmates to help me cut through all that red tape, so I had to find my own way through. That is the only time I used it."

"I was wondering how you had so many different classes loaded onto your tablet. The higher ups like to keep the learning rather segmented, even though having people cross-train would be a lot more efficient. A holdover from the Empire, I guess."

"I know, right? We have redundancies built into everything, why not have redundancies in our training?"

"That's it! Redundancies!" Dean exclaimed.

"What about them?"

"When there is a new iteration of the system put in place, the previous ones are stored in the backup systems, along with any information deemed pertinent. If we can find a way to restore it to one of the older versions, we can still find the information we need without having to cut through as much security. And if we put that older version on a mirror machine we can try again with a different iteration if we fail. The setup will slow things down somewhat, but if we are smart about it, this could save a lot of time in the long run."

"Let's do it, then. How do I help?" Grace asked.

"Bring me any non-networked machines you have available, and if you don't mind, I could use some more pain meds. My arm is starting to hurt again."

"Oh yeah, of course. I'll grab some rations too. I get the feeling that it's going to be a long night."

That was an understatement.

Day 34

"There has to be something we missed," Grace muttered, staring at the screen as if her glare would force the computer to give up its answers. Dean sighed, leaning back in his chair, rubbing his eyes.

"There are plenty of hints and clues but not enough to prove anything," he groaned. "What I wouldn't give for a back door into Lucas's account."

"What would you need for that?"

"I can do a lot with a little. Unfortunately, he was way too smart to give me anything to go on. Anything he contacted me through came out clean as a whistle."

"Could you use the messages he sent me?"

"That depends entirely on where he sent them from. Mind if I take a look?"

"Sure. Here."

She unlocked her tablet and pulled up the messenger program that Lucas contacted her through most frequently.

"Huh. He is persistent, I'll give him that. This isn't an account he tried to contact me through...and it looks like he sent you a message that got interrupted by the crash. I might be able to use that..."

If that sentence had an ending, Dean quickly lost track of it as he started tugging at whatever thread he had found.

"I am going to stretch my legs, go check on the water treatment. Give me a call if you need anything," Grace said.

He nodded, not looking up as she left the room.

She whiled away the following hours, checking on things around the ships and ensuring that Dean continued to hydrate while he worked. Occasionally he called her in to help with something but for the most part, she gave him the space and support he needed to work his magic.

"Dean, you get twenty more minutes than I am making you take a break," Grace called. "It'll be dark in a few hours and we both need some rest."

"I've almost got it. Just double checking a few things, make sure I have the full picture," Dean replied.

"What have you found?" She sat down in the chair next to him, trying to peer over his shoulder at the computer screen.

"Nothing good. Lucas's position put him in contact with the people in charge of ship maintenance, and he gave direct orders to the people who failed to fix our ships. It doesn't necessarily prove that he's responsible for what happened but it's a strong possibility. I would need to see their conversations to be sure. It also looks like he's been in contact with someone outside of the Fleet. He's got it encrypted and I can't seem to crack it."

"If it's a conspiracy with multiple people involved, what are the chances that they use the same encryption codes?"

"It's definitely a possibility. Why?"

"Here, let me try something."

Dean slid out of the way and gestured for Grace to take over. She opened up his decryption program and entered a string of letters and numbers. It didn't work. She tried again. It almost worked.

"Third time's the charm?" Dean shrugged. Grace grimaced and tried again. The screen froze and lagged and for a moment she was afraid it would crash.

Then, slowly, the conversation started to decrypt, and she let out the breath she had been holding.

"How?" he asked.

"I got partnered with the guy Lucas was talking to for a project and he had a little song for it. At first, I was annoyed but now I am glad he did, because otherwise I wouldn't have remembered it."

"Have I told you lately that you're amazing?" Dean said, flashing Grace a wry smile.

She smiled back, bumping her shoulder against his. "If I had a credit for every time, I'd have enough to buy myself a really nice dinner back home."

"When we get back somewhere that has real food, the first meal is on me. Hell, I'll even get the first round of drinks."

"We have to get off this planet first, then find a way to avoid being court-martialed. One step at a time."

"It still stands, and you can hold me to it."

"Sure thing, Dean. Looks like this is going to take a while and it'll be nightfall soon. What do you say we watch a movie?"

"A movie sounds great. Why don't you get it all set up, and I'll tidy things up here?"

"Don't take too long, okay? And don't forget to take your meds."

"Yes, ma'am."

When he joined her in the media room, she had one of the larger sections of furniture pulled down from the wall.

"I figured since one of us is usually asleep before the credits end, we may as well be comfortable," Grace explained. "Plus, I trust you and honestly, I wouldn't mind a little physical contact. So long as you are comfortable with it, and we keep it friendly."

"Of course. I promise to keep my hands to myself and if you set a boundary, I will respect it."

"Good, and I will do the same."

"Excellent. What are we watching?"

"One of my favorites from when I was a kid growing up. Mom would always play it for me when I was sick, so I've been wanting to play it for you, even though you are mostly better."

"Mostly better, not all better. Who knows, this movie could be what pushes me into the well category."

"That's not how it works but I appreciate the enthusiasm. Now hush, it's movie time."

They started out with a foot of space between them, but by the time the movie hit the turning point, it had shrunk to a few inches and Dean had his uninjured arm stretched out behind Grace's head.

They made it through the first movie just fine. They did not make it through the second.

Dean woke up just long enough to turn off the screen before the third movie could start. Grace stirred briefly, but she did not wake. Instead, she turned and snuggled closer to him before settling into an even deeper sleep. He brushed a loose strand of hair out of her face, momentarily mesmerized.

They may have only known each other for a short time, but he found himself caring for her and trusting her more than he thought possible. Sure, he had friends, but this was different. She had saved him in more ways than one, and she was only in this situation because of him. He brushed the gentlest of kisses against her forehead, then pulled the blanket closer around her before drifting back off to sleep.

Personal log, Dean Lindsay

The first time I had my heart broken, I was fifteen years old. It seems so silly now, looking back, but I thought it was the end of the world. Little did I know that something worse awaited me in the following year.

I don't remember much about the breakup anymore, but I remember what dad said to me afterward. It didn't make any sense to the love struck young teenage me, but now, in my current situation, it is starting to.

He said that a life well lived is going to be one full of disappointment. When you go after something you want, something you've dreamed about, it doesn't always work out. That's okay though. It gives you something to learn from, a chance to grow once you heal from the pain. Take the time you need to grieve and learn what you need to learn.

He said I promise you, son, that you have so many things to look forward to. It may not feel like it, but your future is so bright. You have your whole life ahead of you to fill with joy and adventure and people who love you. There will be a day when this heartbreak stops hurting and you will be glad that things turned out the way they did. I know I sure am. I thought I would never love again before I met your mother. Now I can't imagine my life without her.

Healing from the breakup was easy. Healing from their loss was harder. But I think I am finally hitting the point in my life where the pain will start to fade. I know it will never go away, but I will keep growing and keep moving. I am going to be okay.

I will rebuild my life into the one I want to live, and no matter what, I will make sure Grace is a part of it. I honestly can't imagine it otherwise. She's the best thing that ever happened to me, and I know that together, we will work past the hurt this mess has caused and find something better.

It is going to be okay. We will be okay.
Damn, I miss my dad.

Day 35

Grace woke feeling far more rested and far more comfortable than she had in a very long time. She rolled onto her back and stretched her arms wide, accidentally smacking Dean in the face and nearly jostling his broken arm.

"Woah, watch the face," he said.

"Oh my gosh, I am so sorry. I forgot..."

"It's okay, you're all good. No harm done."

She sat up and stared at his face, reading past his initial surprise to the look that had been on his face before she nearly hit it. "Dean, what's wrong? Are you in pain? Are you sick?"

"Easy, Grace. Physically I am fine, not counting the broken arm and the itchy scars."

"Then why are you so pale? I know something's up. It's written all over your face."

He sighed, pushing himself into a sitting position. With his now free arm, he pulled the tablet out from under his cast.

"The decryption program finished a few hours ago. The picture it paints...let's just say it's not pretty. Grace, the leadership has been lying to everyone. The Fleet didn't leave to lead the Imperial forces away from Arcadius, not really. That's just the story they spread to get everyone to play along. That's why communications have been so strictly controlled and compartmentalized, and why most ships are operating with a skeleton crew. It's also why we are so off track from where we should be."

"Because we aren't going to the Myron asteroid belt." The pieces were starting to fit together in Grace's mind but whatever picture they made, she wasn't sure she wanted to see it.

"Because Lucas is leading us back to the Empire. Through Jump Point Tarsis. And as of a few days ago, he has the whole Fleet on lockdown, so whoever knows can't do anything to stop it."

"Well. Shit."

"Yep." Both reactions felt inadequate, but then again Dean didn't really know what to do with the revelation. Everyone they ever knew or loved was in danger, and they could very well be the only two people who knew about it.

"What are we going to do?" Grace asked, steel creeping back into her voice.

"Haven't the foggiest," Dean admitted.

"We have to tell people."

"Of course, but how? We are stranded and don't have enough evidence."

"We get off this planet and we find some proof. People deserve to know the truth of what's going on with the Fleet. They deserve the chance to make their own decisions."

"Back to repairs, then. I have some ideas for how to get both ships ready to fly without having to completely overhaul the *Borealis*' hull. If I can swap around some of the panels, we can keep the compromised sections contained to areas that can function without active life support. It does mean we will have to do a spacewalk to repair anything, but we will be able to fly."

"We also need to figure out where we need to go. Do we go after the Fleet, or do we go back to the rebellion?" Grace asked.

"I...honestly don't know. One problem at a time. I can probably rig the beacon to send a signal back to where the Council ships are coming from, asking for a pickup. They may know more than we do, and we can always trade the information we have gathered so far for them not throwing us in the brig."

"Oh yeah, they're going to look at us as turncoats, even though we didn't exactly know what was really going on…I knew joining the Fleet was going to keep me busy, but I had no idea it was going to make my life so complicated."

"Wishing you never signed on?" Dean asked.

"Do I wish I had known what I was getting into when I joined? Maybe. But then again, I always wanted to be somewhere I could make a difference, and this seems like a pretty good chance. Who knows what they could have gotten away with if we hadn't been here?"

"Sounds like it's up to us to make sure they don't succeed."

"Back to the to-do list, then." Grace pulled out her tablet and pulled up the list. "Which just got longer."

"My dad always said nothing worth doing would be easy."

"Sounds just like my mom."

They had the beacon reconfigured by nightfall, broadcasting a signal back towards what they hoped was the rebellion. With that done, Dean was content to take it easy, but Grace had too much pent-up nervous energy to relax. She fluttered about the ships, fussing over every little thing, unable to stop moving until Dean gently grabbed her hands, bringing her pacing to a standstill.

"Grace, you are making me tired just watching you. I know you want to keep working but there is nothing we can do right now," he said softly.

"I can't just sit and do nothing."

"I didn't say you had to. We just need another way to get the nervous energy out."

"And what do you suggest?"

"Dance party. You said it yourself, music can be therapeutic, and dancing is a really good way to wear off some energy. I even have the perfect music for it. Come on, just give it a try. Fifteen minutes is all I ask and if that doesn't work, we can do something else."

"Fine," she relented.

Dean gave her hands a squeeze before dropping them and heading over to the console. They were on the *Prism,* and he had already shared a large portion of his library with her. It took him a few seconds to find the playlist he wanted, but as the first song began to echo through the halls, a smile spread across Grace's face.

She danced rather reluctantly until the beat increased, then she started to lose herself in the sound and the movement. Dean had the volume just loud enough to drown out thought without endangering their hearing, and between the first and second song he adjusted the settings, so the bass vibrated the floor beneath their feet.

They danced and sang late into the night, partying like they had never had the chance to before, until tiredness won out. They collapsed into their usual seats in the helm, staring up into the starlit sky that had become so very familiar over the past weeks.

"Thanks, Dean. I didn't realize how much I needed that."

"I'm here for you, Grace, and I'm not just saying that because we are literally stuck here together. You're my friend, and I always help my friends," he said, pulling back the other words he was not yet ready to let out.

"I'm glad you're here...I mean, I'm not glad you crash landed here after crashing into me but..."

"I know what you mean, and I feel the same way. Now let's get some sleep. We have a lot of work to do tomorrow."

"Okay. Goodnight, Dean."

"Night, Grace."

Day 36

Hey Mom, looks like I might be coming home later than I thought I would. Dean and I are still on track with our plans to fix the ships, of course. I know you won't be getting this until after I get back home, but writing this out makes me feel better. Especially since I have no idea what is going to happen.

We are most likely not going to be rejoining the Fleet, at least not like I originally planned. There's something going on that's a little hard to explain, but it's something I can't ignore. You always taught me to do the right thing, even when it's hard. Even when it sounds crazy. I can't just sit back and hope someone else fixes this. I have to do something. We have to do something.

It won't be easy. You may hear all sorts of things about me between now and when I make it home. I will make it home, though. I promise. And when I do, I will tell you everything.

Until then, just know that I love you and I will see you again. I promise.

Grace

"This would be a lot faster if I was out there with you," Dean grumbled from his seat inside the ship.

Grace glared at the drone that hovered a few feet off her shoulder.

"You can't wear the suit with the cast on and you aren't clear to take the cast off until the day after tomorrow at the earliest. Now, stop whining and talk me through it. Am I clear to begin removing the panel?"

"Inter-ship airlocks are sealed. *Borealis* readings are coming in clear. You are good to start swapping the panels. You know what to do. I'll keep an eye out if anything goes wrong."

"Glad to know you have my back, Dean."

"Any time, Grace."

The drone drifted backwards as she got to work, methodically removing the damaged panels and replacing them with undamaged panels, one swap at a time. Dean kept her apprised of any changes to the monitoring system, though there were few to be noted. She kept working until she got the alert that her suit's oxygen was low. Then she finished the panel she was working on and re-entered the *Prism*.

"Cutting it close there, Dillard," Dean called from the helm.

"Stuff it, Lindsay. I had it under control. Anything back from our message?"

"Not yet. I made some more adjustments to the positioning and the amplification rate. Hopefully that'll do something."

"Hopefully."

"You did great work out there, by the way. Keep this up and we will be ready to go ahead of schedule," Dean commented.

"If only these suits lasted longer. We will be out of here soon enough, though. Is there anything we can do here in the meantime?"

"I was just thinking that we are going to need some way to communicate with other ships. I don't have the materials to repair both systems, but I can use parts from both to build something functional. I'll need an extra set of hands, though."

"What you need is to rest your arm, so it'll heal," Grace chided. "I've become quite adept at mechanic work, so let me handle the hands-on stuff while you direct."

"Sounds like a plan, though I will need to help you with some of it. It's kind of a two-person job. I promise to be careful, though."

"Deal. Break first, though."

"Break first," he agreed.

She dropped into her usual seat next to Dean, leaning back with one arm draped over her eyes. "Wake me in thirty minutes."

"Will do. Enjoy your nap, Grace."

Silence lapsed over the ship as Dean disappeared into the copious notes he had been taking since they crashed. Even with the careful rationing of their food and water, enough time had passed that they were beginning to run low on both. Neither had openly addressed the issue, but both noticed the other skipping meals, to the point where they started splitting them. He did the math over and over again, yet each time the picture it painted was not a pretty one. Short of the Fleet sending back a streaker, which he knew they wouldn't, help would not come from them in time. That left whoever the Council might have sent to follow.

He ran through different iterations of the conversation that would come from that meeting in his head, trying to craft the responses most likely to keep Grace safe. They may decide to hold him responsible for the actions of his adopted family, and they certainly wouldn't be inclined to trust him. He had suspected too many things for too long and done nothing to stop them. Grace was right. He was a coward. But for her, he would be brave.

She stirred before he had time to wake her, and as she flashed him a smile he pasted on an even bigger smile in return. He would do anything for her.

"So, what's your brilliant plan for fixing the radio?" she prodded.

"Well, our ships have different radio builds, but I am pretty sure the parts are compatible and if we add the pieces from the beacon, we can fashion something that will, at the very least, allow us to get short messages out."

"Great. Where do we start?"

Dean pulled up the schematics for both ships on the console in front of him and started talking Grace through his plan to link the two radio communication bays through the airlock. It would take a few hours, leaving no daylight left for other tasks, but he was confident it could be done.

"...and then tomorrow we can get back to the hull repairs," he said.

"Once again, you amaze me with your technical brilliance. One important question, though. Will you be able to breathe on your ship?" Grace asked.

"I should be able to. I adjusted the room seals, but I've also been charging up the breathers as well, just in case."

"Excellent. Don't want you getting any more hurt."

"At least if I did, I know I have an excellent doctor to take care of me."

"Please, don't make me do that again. That was so stressful."

"I promise I will endeavor to keep myself safe, so I don't cause you any further distress."

"Good. Now shoo. We have work to do."

Dean did as he was told, chuckling along the way to pick up his tools and a breather. As they worked, they couldn't help but discuss the implications of what they had discovered. The news would impact a lot of people, and there would be no avoiding the chaos and turmoil that followed. They also had to come to terms with the fact that however things shook out, they would be caught squarely in the middle.

"What if someone from the Fleet gets here first?" Grace asked.

"They won't."

"But what if they do?"

"Then we tell them the truth and show them the evidence we've collected. Unless we think they're loyal to the Empire, then we play dumb."

"And what if they're from the rebellion? How are we supposed to convince them of something we are barely convinced of ourselves?"

"Well, I don't know about you but with what we've been able to find I can't think of a single other explanation for what is going on that isn't completely unhinged. We have Lucas' private conversation with the person we assume is his Imperial handler and we have the records that prove our ships were sabotaged. We have also effectively been left for dead by the rest of the Fleet. I am pretty sure we can convince whoever answers our distress call to give us the benefit of the doubt at the very least. There isn't much point in worrying, though, until we have some sign that there is going to be a response. So, let's focus on what we can control, okay?"

"Okay," Grace relented. "I'm just...I can't shake the feeling that we are missing something. If we both posed that much of a threat to whatever is going on, wouldn't someone have put a failsafe in place to ensure we didn't live long enough to tell anyone the truth?"

"I've thought about that too. Trust me, if they had any backups, they've already been dealt with. I have been over every inch of both ships and every line of code," Dean said. "We are as safe as we can be right now."

"Alright. I trust you. I realize my paranoia is irrational..."

"That is totally fine, Grace. There's a lot going on. I've got your back, though."

"And I've got yours."

His words didn't completely erase her anxiety, but they did soothe her mind enough to allow her to focus on the task at hand. The work steadied her, helped calm the fears that kept raging in the back of her mind. They would take things one step at a time. They were going to be okay.

Personal log, Dean Lindsay

I told Grace about the code I found buried deep in both of our ships' systems, the failsafe to prevent us from leaving the planet. I have scrubbed it as thoroughly as I can and checked regularly to make sure it hasn't come back. Thankfully, whoever created it wasn't quite that clever.

It scares me, though, the ease with which Lucas was able to remove the two of us from the equation. There are powerful people involved in this deception and if we aren't careful about how we shine the light on it, a lot of people could get hurt.

I try not to think about the ripple effect this news is going to have. The rebellion has been struggling enough to build itself a home. Now they will have to face the reality that there are loyalists in their ranks. Loyalists who could easily ruin everything.

But I can't think about that right now. It's like Grace says: take things one step at a time and one day you will touch the stars.

Day 37

The updated radio started getting a signal the following morning, but the connection was sporadic at best.

"How long until we get a clearer signal?" Grace asked.

"No way to tell," Dean admitted, though he wished he had a better answer. "I have a few tricks I can try but there's only so much I can do without the source coming closer."

"In that case, I am going to get back to work on the hull while the light is nice. I can also double check the comms equipment."

"You're amazing."

"I know." She tossed a dazzling smile over her shoulder that warmed a certain place in Dean's chest, causing his face to flush. Thankfully, she didn't see this, or he would have blushed all the more at her teasing. Or maybe she would have started blushing too. So far, they had both been dancing around any possible implications of their growing comradery.

She suited up and grabbed her pack of tools, which she had commandeered from Dean. Not that he protested much when she did so. In fact, he claimed that she was the best assistant he ever had, not that he would admit to actually having had assistants before. She found she enjoyed the work, though, and in light of all the uncertainty, she needed to feel like she was accomplishing something.

The little drone bobbed after her as she walked around the ships to the section of the *Borealis* that she had marked the day before as needing to be exchanged. She fell into herself as she went through the familiar movements, singing under her breath as she methodically worked through her tasks.

After the first panel was removed, she caught the telltale sounds of Dean singing along, though he sang so softly the microphone only picked up snippets.

"Don't be shy now," she teased, starting up a new song even louder than before. Dean laughed and joined in, loud and dramatic and silly. On the next song things quickly devolved into some made up medley of different genres stacked on top of each other and somehow wrapped up in a call and response that should not have worked as well as it did. "Not bad, Dean. If engineering doesn't work out, you have a career in music."

"Appreciate the vote of confidence, Grace. That'll be one of my first releases."

"Oh no, I am not doing that again."

"It's okay, you don't have to. I recorded it."

Grace paused in the middle of loosening a bolt to glare in the direction she knew Dean was, even though he could not see her. "You didn't."

"I did."

"If you even think about sending that to anyone, I will put laxatives in all of your food."

"Ouch. Are you sure you want to do that to yourself? We do live in rather close quarters."

"Fine, I will find some other way to make you suffer. Don't test me, Dean."

"I promise, on my honor, not to reveal this recording to anyone without your permission. That said, I am absolutely making a copy for my own enjoyment and there is nothing you can do to stop me."

"You're the worst," Grace teased, going back to her work. He laughed and let the conversation drop, leaving her to try desperately to ignore the sound of him replaying the recording. It honestly wasn't too bad, but it still felt embarrassing, and she had no interest in sharing it with anyone else. She found, though, that him keeping a copy didn't bother her too much. It was a fond memory, after all, and one she would also be interested in reliving.

"Hey, Grace, how's it looking out there?" Dean asked, breaking her mental wandering.

"I am almost done with the last panel exchange, then I was going to check the comms equipment. Unless you need me to do that later."

"Just focus on the panels, then come back inside. I need your help with something."

"Okay," Grace said, lining up one of the bolts to secure the intact panel.

When Dean said nothing else, she grew nervous. Dean took great joy in explaining his ideas and discussing the ins and outs of engineering with her. It wasn't often that he went quiet like that. Something was up, and she wanted very much to know what. She also wanted to leave this planet sooner, rather than later.

So, she finished the panel and applied the sealant around the edges before packing up her tools and heading back onto the ship.

"Honey, I'm home," she called as she stepped out of the airlock. "What's got you so excited?"

"We got a response on the radio. At least, I think it was a response. Communications are garbled at this distance, but I think they got our mayday because they signaled back that they are approaching."

"Are they with the Council or the Fleet?"

"Didn't say but given where the signal came from its most likely Council. And they seem…friendly. Won't know anything for sure until tomorrow at the earliest."

"When will they get here?"

"Not sure. Two, maybe three days? Either way I'd feel a lot more comfortable knowing that we have our own way off this rock," Dean said.

"Yes. Options. Options are good. Not being alone is also good. I mean...you know."

"Yeah, I know. As much as I've enjoyed your company, I still look forward to the possibility of being around other people. Especially with the stuff we figured out these past few days."

"What all do we have left to do before we are ready to go?" Grace asked.

"Well, even with the repairs to the hull of the *Borealis* I am still not confident that it will be safe to be onboard. I'd suggest moving anything of importance onto the *Prism* just in case something happens, and we have to jettison the *Borealis*. I am pretty sure between the two of us we can finish fixing the radio on the *Prism* to operate separately. That is, assuming you are comfortable sharing your ship with me."

"Yeah, like you haven't moved in already," Grace laughed. "May as well make it official. Pick a room and it's yours. I can help you get all your belongings moved over. Then we can get to work on the comms."

"Sounds like a plan."

They celebrated their new cohabitation with candy and cartoons, curled up together on the bed with a fuzzy blanket thrown over them. Grace fell asleep curled up next to Dean and woke up hours later with his arm wrapped around her waist. The touch was unexpected but not entirely unwelcome, she found, and she drifted off back to sleep once more.

Day 38

"How much longer until we know if the changes to the radio worked?" Grace asked. She and Dean had finished their tinkering and rearranging a few hours ago, leaving them with not much to keep them occupied outside of lessons and reading. It did very little to decrease the anticipation.

"It's sending out the same message that was going yesterday," Dean repeated. "The only thing we can do is wait for them to reach out again. According to everything I've read about those radio systems, what we did should work."

"Do you think something could have happened to them? Maybe they decided not to investigate our signal."

"That is possible. And that is why we have been working to make sure we can leave on our own if we need to. It's going to be okay, Grace. We've got this."

"I'm spiraling again, sorry. I'm just so bored. I want them to reach out already."

"Me too. If you want to walk around the ship, stretch your legs and get some of the anxiety energy out, I can stay here and give you a shout if anything happens."

"Nah, I think I'll just read. If I start walking around, I might pace a hole in the floor."

"Fair enough." Dean watched out of the corner of his eye as Grace leaned back in her chair, tablet in hand. She sometimes looked the happiest when she was reading. He propped his feet in the seat next to him, focusing his attention back on the scanners.

To help the time pass faster, they took turns selecting music and books to listen to. Grace even threw in a couple of classes on things such as music and art history. They took walks about the ship, then a walk outside of the ship to get some sunshine and collect some more samples. Grace then taught Dean some new tricks when it came to studying different materials and testing the compatibility of certain minerals. Then they both got distracted talking about what would need to be done to get a hydroponic garden set up on one of the ships, so they could grow their own food. This was all theoretical, of course, since nothing on the planet had proven edible so far.

That didn't mean they couldn't find some way to counteract any ill effects those plants may have on their bodies. As their rations continued to dwindle, they had to think of something. They could only split and skip so many meals before they started to suffer from lack of nutrients.

"It's a good thing I downloaded those classes on horticulture and adaptive farming," Grace commented. "Everyone said they would never have a practical application for my work, but here we are."

"Here we are indeed. I had a feeling that you would be the one responsible for helping us survive. I can fix things, sure, but you can create them."

"Don't you go discounting your worth, Dean. This has been a team effort, and you are every bit as responsible for our survival as I am. I would absolutely be dead without your help." Grace reached over and patted his hand, giving it a gentle squeeze before pulling it back.

Dean smiled. "We are in this together, Grace."

"That we are. And there's no other person I'd rather have my back."

Personal Log, Dean Lindsay

This is going to sound crazy, but I need to get this thought out of my head, so here it is.

I wish we didn't have to leave this planet. Logically I know there is no way we can stay here. We don't have enough supplies to sustain ourselves for much longer and we have to make sure people know what's really going on with the Fleet. I know that.

But I wish we could stay. This planet has started to grow on me. It's so beautiful and new and quiet. I don't need to worry about playing the part that the family wants me to play.

That doesn't change the fact that we need to leave, and we need to leave soon. There is a truth that needs to get out and we may very well be the only people who can tell it. That puts us in a position where we can do a lot of good and save a lot of lives. It also puts us right smack dab in the middle of the fallout.

One way or another, things are going to get messy. I will take as much of the heat as I can. I promised to keep Grace safe and get her home. I will keep that promise.

Day 40

Personal Log, Grace Dillard

All this waiting is going to drive me crazy. I need to know one way or another who it is that is coming to get us so I can get my brain to stop feeding me never-ending nightmare scenarios. I keep imagining all the terrible things that might happen if the loyalists in the Fleet were able to get their hands on us. The fear of the unknown can be the most difficult fear to deal with because it is unknown.

I need something to lean on. Something to hold on to. Dean has been keeping me steady for a while now. I don't know what I would do without him. But I can tell that even he is starting to unravel a bit. Maybe I can keep myself together by helping him keep it together.

We are a team, after all. One way or another, we will get through this.

Aside from brief bursts of static, they didn't hear from their potential rescuers again. Grace nearly lost herself in a spiral of anxiety, but Dean managed to pull her back. In doing so, he also avoided falling to his own inner demons that begged him to give up and accept the fact they would never be leaving this planet.

On the dawn of the 40th day, the work was done, and the final round of checks were completed.

"So, we can leave?" Grace asked.

"It looks like it. Everything is coming back green, and we have enough energy stored in the backup generators to keep us going for a while, so long as we are careful not to waste any. I say we wait until the last of the auxiliary power cells are charged, then head out."

"That is an excellent idea, especially considering how much power we will burn through just leaving the atmosphere."

"Precisely, and we can recharge any excess depletion while we get a lay of the space around us. That'll give us time to get a course plotted for wherever we decide to go."

"I wish we could just go home. I miss my mom."

"I don't think we can go home just yet," Dean said gently. "Not until we know what's really going on and know that the truth is out. I promise you, though, I will do everything in my power and beyond to make sure you get home once this is all over. I look forward to meeting your mom."

Grace reached over and grabbed his hand, giving it a gentle squeeze. He held on when she started to pull away and she decided to just let him keep it. She only needed one hand to watch her lessons anyway. During her time of playing emergency doctor, she had caught up to him when it came to long-term medical treatment methods, so they had started working through the classes together.

If nothing else, it helped pass the time and gave them something new to talk about.

They had paused their learning to split a quick lunch and go through the pre-flight checklist one more time when a shadow settled over the ship. At first this did not concern them very much, since clouds would occasionally drift over the sun. Then Dean noticed that the thrum of the engine had changed slightly.

Then he realized it wasn't the engine, but something outside of the ships that changed the timbre of the thrumming.

"I don't think we're alone," he whispered. "There's another ship nearby, possibly above us."

Something knocked on the door of the *Borealis*.

"Did they identify themselves on approach?" Grace asked.

"No. They must be using some kind of cloaking. How do we want to play this?"

The outsider knocked again.

"Let me make the introduction," Grace said after a few seconds of consideration. "You hide somewhere nearby, in case they decide to try anything. I will figure out who they are and what they are doing in this system."

"Are you sure? Why not let me make the approach? I don't like the idea of you putting yourself in harm's way."

Grace fixed him with a mock-scathing look, and he put his hands up in mock-surrender. "I'm not the one with a broken arm and I won't be in danger if you are nearby to provide backup. Plus, people are much more likely to underestimate me."

Dean knew better than to argue with that.

"I would never, but then again, I feel like I know you better than most. Where do you want me?"

"Just find a nearby room and take this." She handed him a flare gun. "They give them to us for when we do field work. It's not the best aim but it can be very distracting. At the very least it will buy us time if things get messy."

He took the flare gun and tucked it into his sling, which mostly concealed it. The cast may have been gone but Grace insisted he use the sling to not re-injure himself. They walked into the *Borealis* and she waited until he was hidden in one of the rooms to put on her breather and open the airlock. Two suited figures stood outside, one male and one female. The male was the only one obviously armed.

"Hello," the woman said. "My name is Carla, and I'm the captain of the *Nova*. We received your distress signal. Permission to come aboard?"

"Permission granted. You can leave your weapon in the airlock. I promise, you are safe here," Grace said. The woman turned to the man and nodded. They followed Grace onto the *Borealis* and, to Grace's relief, the man left his gun by the door. Sure, they could have other weapons on their persons but at the very least they weren't being outwardly hostile.

Grace led them into the room next to the one Dean occupied, giving him the chance to listen in to the conversation. The room also had a table and chairs, making it a logical choice outside of that fact.

"You can remove your helmets. The life support is fully functional, and we will get an alert if something goes wrong." Grace removed her breather to prove her point. Carla removed her helmet, with the man following suit soon after.

"If you don't mind my getting straight to business, how did you end up stranded here?" Carla asked.

"I was traveling with the Fleet when there was an engine malfunction that resulted in my crash landing here. I have been repairing my ship in the meantime, while waiting to see if anyone picked up my distress signal," Grace answered.

"So, you are part of the Arcadius Fleet? Where were you headed?"

"The Myron Belt."

"Is that so?" the woman said. "You are a fair bit off course to be heading to the Myron Belt. Why were you headed there?"

Grace shifted uncomfortably in her seat, unsure how to respond. "What's your connection to the Fleet?" she asked finally.

"Oh, I know a few people who joined up a while ago. Haven't really heard from them since. That's part of why we just had to come investigate your distress signal. There's no real reason for anyone to be out this way, especially not alone."

"She's not alone," Dean said, stepping into the doorway.

Grace shot him a harsh look, surprised and upset by his sudden appearance. The man immediately took up a defensive position between Dean and Carla as she spun around to see who it was that had spoken.

"Identify yourself," the man demanded.

"The name is Dean Lindsay, former Lieutenant of the Arcadius Fleet. I believe your captain might be familiar with me." Dean held his hands up to show he was unarmed.

"Did you say Lindsay?" Carla said incredulously. She stood and moved around the man to get a better look. "Well damn, you got tall."

"I thought I recognized your voice. You sound so much like your mom," Dean commented.

"Excuse me, what is going on here?" Grace asked.

"Our parents went to school together back on the generation ships," Carla explained. "They stayed friends after landing, so we more or less grew up together for a while there. Us and a bunch of other kids."

"Yeah, I grew up in a pretty tight community. Haven't seen Carla here in ages, though."

"How did the two of you end up here?" Carla gestured between Grace and Dean.

"It's a bit of a long story. You could say that one of my benefactors decided the Fleet would be better off without us in it," Dean replied.

"And what is the rest of the story?" Carla prodded.

"Grace and I were getting close to an uncomfortable truth, so my dearest brother Lucas decided to kill two birds with one stone, I guess. Didn't quite work out, though, because we survived and together were able to piece together exactly what the Aemaris family are trying to hide."

"Which is?" the man asked.

"The Fleet is heading to Jump Point Tarsis to rejoin the Empire," Grace said, "and only a select few are aware of this. Everyone else believes that we were headed for the asteroid field to deal with the so-called Imperials on our tail."

"There are hundreds of people who are being force-fed a steady diet of propaganda and have no idea what is really going on," Dean continued. "We just figured it out ourselves and have been trying to find a way off this planet."

"Do you have any proof?" Carla asked.

"We have some evidence, but it may not be substantial enough to be considered solid proof. We would need access to the Fleet databases to get that," Dean said.

The man gestured at Carla to step out into the hallway.

"If you will excuse us for just one second," she said politely.

"By all means." Dean gestured toward the door. The man stepped out first, followed by Carla, and from the sounds of their footsteps they traveled a few feet down the hall before stopping to have a whispered conversation.

"Are you sure we can trust them?" Grace whispered to Dean.

"Carla is good people," Dean replied.

"Okay. I trust your judgment."

"Thanks, and I understand your hesitation. I probably shouldn't have sprung that on you like that."

"It's alright. I was starting to flounder anyway. Do you think they'll help us?"

"Oh, without a doubt. Some of the others might be suspicious of us, but she will make sure we are safe."

"Good. That's good. I'd like to be out of here."

"Likewise," Dean said.

He sat down next to Grace, and she instinctively reached for his hand under the table. He squeezed her fingers before threading his through them, resting the back of her hand against his knee. A few minutes later, Carla returned.

"Apologies, Shutz here had some concerns he needed to express but never fear, I have convinced him that you are trustworthy. The fact is, we were sent to figure out exactly what is going on with the Fleet and to see if we can find a way to resolve things peacefully. It wasn't until now that we had anything close to the full picture, and if what you're saying is true, then we need to stop it. I would certainly appreciate your help, but I also understand if you'd rather just go home. We can provide some aid but I'm afraid we can't stay long. We need to catch up with the Fleet," Carla said.

"What do you plan to do?" Grace asked.

"Aside from catching up to them? We will need to find a way onboard one of the ships so we can figure out what exactly is going on and how to stop whatever they're planning. If you are right and most of the Fleet doesn't know about the end goal, then maybe spreading the truth can tip the scales. We won't know until we get there."

"I'll go with you," Dean said. "I can give you a copy of what we already have, but you are going to need my help. I am good with tech, and I know Lucas better than most people."

"I appreciate the offer. It'll be nice to have something in my back pocket that he will never expect."

"I am coming too," Grace said.

"Grace, are you sure? You said you wanted to go home."

"I fully intend to, but I can't very well sit back and do nothing while all my friends are in danger. I joined the Fleet wanting to make a difference, to do something good. I'm going."

"Very well, then. The good news is we are traveling on a big ship that can carry smaller ships, since I noticed this one has sustained a bit of damage. We can tow the other. It may not be the most comfortable of quarters and there will be danger once we approach the Fleet, but I promise we will do our best to keep both of you safe," Carla said.

"When do we leave?" Grace asked.

"As soon as you are ready."

Working together, the crews managed to get the *Prism* and the *Borealis* safely into the cargo bay before nightfall. Grace and Dean were immediately quarantined under orders of Mingo, the ship's medic, due to prolonged exposure to foreign elements.

"Is there any way I can send a message to my mom?" Grace asked. "I just want to let her know I'm okay. No details and I'll keep it short."

Mingo glanced toward the hallway Shutz had disappeared down. "Write the message and where to send it. I'll run it by Shutz and make sure he sends it."

"Thank you."

Message from UNKNOWN to Kara Dillard.

- Decrypting message -

- Message decrypted -

Hey Mom, it's Grace. I know you haven't heard from me in a while and I'm sorry about that. Things have been complicated, and I don't see that changing for a while. I wish I could tell you everything but it's safer if I keep some things to myself. I just wanted to let you know that I am okay. I am safe. I really wish I could come home, but there is something I need to take care of first.

I promise, the next time I see you I will explain everything. Until then, just trust that I am doing the right thing and know that I love you lots.

I'll be home soon. I just need to touch the stars first.

- End message. Do Not Reply -

Day 45

Lucas Aemaris sat at his desk in his private quarters aboard the *Supernova*, flagship of the Arcadius Fleet, waiting for an update from his point of contact in the Empire. The appointed meeting time had come and gone, but apparently things had been getting interesting on their side, so Lucas chose to wait, if only to prove himself the more responsible one. He also needed to know if the removal of his brother and the possible exposure of their true destination had any impact on the plans. The news had already been delivered to his contact, of course, but he still had yet to hear a response about how to proceed.

Incoming transmission...please enter decryption password.

Lucas typed in the day's decryption code.

Decrypting...

UNKNOWN: Can you confirm the problem has been resolved?

Lameris: Yes.

UNKNOWN: Can you confirm that the breach has been contained?

Lameris: Both parties have been removed from the equation.

UNKNOWN: If any of this information proves to be incorrect, the punishment shall fall on you.

Lameris: I am aware of the expectations. What I would like to know is if this changes the plan at all. I still have total control of the Fleet.

UNKNOWN: We are moving up the timetable. You will find the details attached. You are expected to adjust accordingly.

Lameris: I will. For the glory of the Empire.

UNKNOWN: For the glory of the Empire.
   -CONNECTION TERMINATED-

About the author

LS DERRIN

L.S. Derrin is a lover of the stars and a lover of stories. Growing up on Star Wars and Star Trek (and eventually, Mass Effect and other beloved sci-fi franchises) has shaped both their reading habits and inspired them to write their own stellar tales.

They currently have three different sci-fi universes living in their head but who knows, maybe one day they will find a way to combine them. The only way to know for sure is to keep reading.

Made in the USA
Coppell, TX
15 February 2026